Where Are My
72 Virgins?

Where Are My 72 Virgins?

Karan Oberoi

PARTRIDGE
A Penguin Random House Company

To order additional copies of this book, contact
Partridge India
000 800 10062 62
orders.india@partridgepublishing.com

www.partridgepublishing.com/india

Contents

Dedication

To all my online chat friends, especially Himangi, Rashmi, Mannat, Shilpa, Disha, Amarpreet and last but also the everlasting Shweta Umdekar who did not relent until she became Shweta Oberoi.

Acknowledgements

A big thanks to one and all, who contributed in the realization of this book in any which way ! Additionally, I would like to thank my family for their love and support, especially my wife for nurturing my dream as her own and for being my first reader and critic.

Chapter 1

Me and My Solitude

Life is as complex an endeavour as simple is the word. It can never be defined by breaths and beats alone. For some it is a journey; for others, a halt. Some seek truth here while others are being sought after in search of truth. Life is a bed of roses, but roses are full of thorns. Some lives are fairy tales, but most of them are unfair-y tales all the way.

It was 29 October 2005. Sarojini Nagar Market, one of the busiest in New Delhi, was packed with people on Diwali eve, shopping for the great Indian festival. Some shopped to cash in on the season discounts and offers while others just to indulge in the festive rhapsody. The whole market was adorned with lights and flowers as the people bought clothes, footwear, toys, gifts, decorative lights, and candles from the shops that tried their best to lure the customers in amid a fierce competition. A young couple with their three-year-old son and a maid stopped by a food vendor to grab a quick bite after shopping unceasingly for hours. Their hands were full of shopping bags, and there wasn't any room for one extra. While they were busy munching, their son extricated his hand from the grip of the maid and ran across the street, allured by a balloon seller. The maid ran

1

behind him to catch hold of the unruly boy as he could have easily disappeared in the crowd like a raindrop in the sea. As the boy reached near the vendor and grabbed a balloon, an explosion across the street gashed through the market teeming with people.

Dinkar Chauhan suddenly wakes up in the middle of the night. He had a bad dream. A picture of his deceased parents covered with a wilted garland of marigold hung on a wall above, overlooking his bed. He grabs a water bottle kept on the side table and deluges his dry throat. With sleep out of the window, he grabs a pen and pad kept adjacent to the bottle and begins to weave his pain in words.

Khandharon mein guzre hue zamaane dhoondte hain,

Hum roz jeene ke naye bahaane dhoondte hain.

I search for the good old days in vestiges of old buildings,

Every day I solicit new excuses to live.

Chhooti uski kalaai aur humne botal thaam li,

Aa jaata hai hosh jahaan, maikhaane dhoondte hain.

Her wrist slipped away from my hand, and I took to booze,

Whenever I come to my senses, I look for a bar.

Kuchh bataane se pehle hi ho jaate hain khaak,

Woh kyaa hai jo shamaa mein parwaane dhoondte hain?

Before revealing anything, they get incinerated,

Why do the moths seek the flame so ardently?

Ghar thaa chhotaa magar, dil mein jagah kaafi thi,

Woh chhote dil waale unche gharaane dhoondte hain.

My house was small, but I had a big heart,

She seeks small-hearted guys with a big house.

Mujhe jalaakar bhi unko chain nahin aayaa,

Ab raakh mein kaunse khazaane dhoondte hain?

She isn't content even after burning me,

What treasure does she seek in my ashes?

Well, that's quite impressive for a sixteen-year-old, isn't it? Though that last couplet reminds me of Ghalib.

Jalaa hai jism jahaan dil bhi jal gayaa hoga,

Kuredte ho jo ab raakh, justjoo kyaa hai?

Where the whole body burnt, heart must have been consumed too,

Now what are you rummaging my ashes for?

What Dinkar writes is not technically a correct ghazal as it is not in meter or *beher*, who cares! Nevertheless, they are still enticing, and that's what matters. The only things that elevate Dinkar out of his despondence are poetry and online chatting. He often expresses his desolation in ghazals, an ancient Persian-Urdu form of poetry in couplets. In a ghazal, each couplet is a complete thought in itself and generally unrelated to the other couplets but sharing a common essence.

Dinkar is depressed, has always been, for life hasn't treated him well. He is sixteen but sour sixteen! What good a childhood bereaved of parental love and an upbringing by an indifferent uncle and aunt possibly had done? Not that Dinkar's uncle and aunt are atrocious or nagging. They tried their best to treat Dinkar like their own son Mayank, but it was Dinkar who chose to estrange himself as he could not accept them as substitute parents. Eventually, his uncle and aunt gave up on him, and now Dinkar lives like a defaulter tenant in his own house and all his uncle and aunt care for is his heirloom.

Dinkar's twelve-by-ten-foot room is the only world he knows, where he spends bulk of his time. The nights haunt him, and he sleeps through the day, much to the annoyance of his aunt.

There is heavy knocking on the door. A husky irritated voice, though of his aunt, calls for him, 'Dinkar, don't you know what time it is? Come down and have your dinner. Whole day this boy is confined to his room, don't know doing what. People think we lock you up and don't let you out. Just learn something from Mayank.'

Dinkar's aunt never lets any opportunity slip through, no matter howsoever infinitesimally small and silly, at hinting what a superior breed Mayank is as compared to Dinkar.

Dinkar reluctantly opens the door as his aunt stands there, glittering under miles of make-up and jewellery. She wears a heavily embroidered red sari on a hefty body, as her blouse appears to pant for air. Her neck gradually got extinct under the weight of her large face. Her bosoms seem to hang from her abdomen instead of her chest, and her waistline and petticoat bury deep under the multiple skinfolds of her belly. She has no reason to be scared of dengue mosquitoes as her obnoxious nose-burning perfume is a deterrent enough. In any case, they won't be able to dig through her thick skin. Only thing missing in her hands is a *var-mala*, or a wedding garland, and she could easily pass for a bride, but one that everyone runs away from. This obsessive-compulsive disorder for apparel is due to the sense of deprivation she had in her early marital life, as Dinkar's uncle wasn't well off to afford all this vanity fair while she saw Dinkar's mother enjoying all the materialistic bliss. Though she has a thing or two to learn about prettification. She looks as if someone has Photoshopped a Caucasian face over an Indian body.

'Come down and take your dinner,' she tells Dinkar, incensed.

'I want to eat chicken or mutton. It's been ages since I had non-veg!' complains Dinkar.

'Oh god, no!' vociferates Aunt as if Dinkar had asked for her kidney. 'Don't you know it's Tuesday? Besides, if you have to eat meat, go out and eat. Until I am alive, no chicken or mutton can enter this house,' Aunt declares her resolution. She is a devout Punjabi woman, and even her husband is not the one to eat and tell.

'Okay, fine! Just wait until 2019 when I'll be an adult. Enough of your caretaking. After that, leave me and my house alone. Phir bas main aur meri tanhai [Then me and my solitude],' replies Dinkar impishly as he lets his aunt in.

Aunt speaks cautiously, 'Beta [Son], I was just saying that you should go out and have fun. We are your own, your flesh and blood. We can't leave you alone in this big house. We care for you. Your uncle will be hurt if he comes to hear this.'

'Sure he will be. It hurts to let go of such a big bungalow,' says Dinkar with a wicked face. 'And please don't wear my mom's jewellery.'

Aunt chooses to ignore as she picks up Dinkar's clothes, spread evenly all over the room, for laundry and hopes Dinkar doesn't intend anything of that sort and just spat it out in rage. Of course, Dinkar isn't serious! He just relishes the look on his foes' faces when he threatens them with ousting. And that's the only arrow he has in his quiver.

Dinkar's house is a two-storey mansion situated at a prime location of Lajpat Nagar in New Delhi, which anyone would be proud to own and stupid to let go. The building is covered with textured brown bricks with quite a few missing here and there while those clinging on are uncertain of their fate as they are getting old. The entrance to premises is through an unwelcoming black vertically grilled iron gate situated on the extreme right of the property. The grills are wide enough for a cat to enter through, though not their own. Actually, there should have been a sign on the gate. 'No dogs but beware of humans inside!'

As you enter from the main gate, though it's highly not recommended, there is a long passageway covered in white marble like most of the older built affluent houses in India boast of. The porch runs right until the end, long enough to park at least two cars which they can't afford. The entry to the living room is through this passage via a small door located few yards from the gate. Dinkar occupies a room on the first floor while the rest of it is uninhabited. FYI, in India, the first floor is the same as the second floor in most countries. We begin with ground floor, first floor, and so on. The houses in the neighbourhood are closely packed to maximize the use of the area as the property rates are higher than the sky. All buildings on the street share walls with the adjacent one, and their roofs are interlinked too, thus providing easy access to the thieves and robbers.

Dinkar's uncle, aunt, cousin, and a maid live on the ground floor while the family also boasts of a non-resident chauffeur. The stairs to Dinkar's room lead from outside the building through the porch, thus leaving him on his own. He is cut off from the rest of the family most of the time, unless he accidentally bumps into them during meals. Still, no words are exchanged, not even smiles, sometimes not even glances.

Dinkar hurriedly goes about his meals while competing with his uncle as to who ignores the other more. Dinkar's uncle is a tiny fellow, almost half the size of his wife but twice her ego and also a couple of inches shorter, who fell prey to the institution of arranged marriages. He has a permanent pout as if trying to hold his tiny moustache between his upper lip and nose. Many a time he has to face the ire of girls and ladies in public places as they think he is advancing to kiss them. Whenever you talk to him, your whole attention is affixed on his moustache as if it will fall off the moment he moves his lips. He works in a clerical position in Public Welfares Department with a reasonable salary but not enough by the standards of the upmarket society he is living in, courtesy of his late brother. This has made him quite stingy over time.

Chapter 2

When Day Meets Night

Dinkar slips into his room after dinner as if the atmosphere outside his chamber weren't conducive to his survival. It's time for him to go online. First he surfs some sites suggesting new ideas for those contemplating suicide, which he notes down for future reference as he sucks big time in committing suicide and failed miserably in his last attempt. One very interesting idea he comes across is to use your body as a conducting medium for AC current between the power source and your television while watching a porn movie and die a horny death.

He logs into a messenger using his ID Aaftaab123 and enters a chat room. The world of Internet chatting is a dicey one. It's a vicious web of incognitos. You never know when one fine day your Eve turns out to be an Adam, and you realize you are so in love with a dude.

Though it doesn't bother Dinkar. All he needs is someone to empathize with. He hasn't been successful yet to make a perennial friend, but it's good that he keeps trying. He sends 'Hi' incessantly for hours to any and every ID but to no avail. Guys just don't want to chat with guys, and girls are ever so busy while the other half are the bots. But today the river is flowing up the mountain. Fortunately or rather unfortunately, he gets a reply from one Kool_Chandni.

Aaftaab123: hi

Kool_Chandni: hi...asl?

Aaftaab123: 16 m delhi, u?

Kool_Chandni: 17 f mumbai

Aaftaab123: how r u?

Kool_Chandni: am fine..howz u?

Aaftaab123: ok

Kool_Chandni: juz ok?

Aaftaab123: ya..wat else?

Kool_Chandni: you sound low dude!

Aaftaab123: am like this only.

Kool_Chandni: so u r not happy?

Aaftaab123: there is nothin to feel happy about.

Kool_Chandni: look around..u'll sure find somethin..life is beautiful..it has so much to offer..take off those gloomy shades you are wearing and see it through my eyes.

Aaftaab123: well u r lucky...I wasn't that fortunate.

Kool_Chandni: y wat happened?

Aaftaab123: I lost my parents when I was 3…before I could have preserved any memories to cherish. Was brought up by my uncle n aunt who care only for my property.

Kool_Chandni: that's sad…but it isn't easy either to dwell on past. try to live in present. its difficult but give it a shot.

Aaftaab123: Well i think i am ensconced in my misery.

Kool_Chandni: oh i see…Hey wats your name?

Aaftaab123: my name is Dinkar Chauhan.

Kool_Chandni: my name is Chandni,..Chandni Khan. What does Dinkar mean?

Aaftaab123: Sun and so does aaftaab…and chandni means moonlight.

Kool_Chandni: I know..so nice combo we make..he he!

Aaftaab123: I am day, you are night. Actually it should have been the other way round.

Kool_Chandni: I fully agree..am bright and cheerful as day, you are dim as night…so tell me mr. sun, wats ur dob?

Aaftaab123: The sinister date..13 dec 2001!

Kool_Chandni: come on buddy…theres no such thing as sinister. Its April 2018 so u r 16 now. Am a bit weak in maths..lol. btw wat a coincidence? mine is 13 dec 2000….n 13 is my lucky number.

Aaftaab123: Really..or u juz tryin to comfort me.

Kool_Chandni: I won't go that far as to change my dob to comfort u! So we both are archers!

Aaftaab123: wat? din get u!

Kool_Chandni: arre sun sign duffer..we both are saggi!!!

Aaftaab123: ya, dats dere. so we must have many things in common.

Kool_Chandni: wat do ya study?

This question has always plagued Dinkar as he could not pass his high school exams and dropped out of school. It is one of the reason for his shying away from the world.

Aaftaab123: 12th..Commerce

Dinkar lies so that Chandni will not frown upon him.

Kool_Chandni: Okk..I m doing B-com. I can give you tutions..ha ha ha.

Aaftaab123: I badly need 'em...lol.

Kool_Chandni: so wat interests u ..hobbies if any!!

Aaftaab123: poetry...I write ghazals.

Kool_Chandni: really...that's great yaar. [buddy]

Kool_Chandni: well I wud luv 2 read them..

Aaftaab123: but most of them have urdu words...u won't understand.

Kool_Chandni: oh really...urdu is in my blood...by the way where did you learn urdu?

Aaftaab123: while watchin movies and listening ghazals.. and internet of course.

Kool_Chandni: great …so lets hear one of your ghazal.

Aaftaab123: but u won't like them. they r sad n depressing.

Kool_Chandni: don u worry..if they r gud, I'll surely like them..now juz type. Irshad! [recite]

Aaftaab123: ok I'll paste one of my favourite composition for u.

Dinkar copies and pastes one of his creations from his personal folder as he eagerly awaits her comments.

In labon pe muskan laayen kaise?

Hum is dil ko samjhayen kaise?

How do I bring a smile on my face?

How should I console my heart?

Ajab si khamoshi hai fiza mein,

Dhadkanon ki siskiyan dabaayen kaise?

There is a strange lull in the atmosphere,

How do I suppress the shrieks of my heartbeats?

Beh gaye ho ashq banke sanam,

Aankhon me tumhe phir basaayen kaise?

You have long been fled in the form of tears,

How do I rehabilitate you again in my eyes?

Dard me mere humdum the jo,

Un zakhmon se juda ho jaayen kaise?

Those who kept me company in my pain,

How do I separate myself from those wounds?

Jaanti hain aankhen raaz dil ke,

Hum zamaane se nazren bachaayen kaise?

Eyes disclose the secrets of the heart,

How should I conceal them from the world?

Andheri hain dil ki raahen 'Aaftaab',

Hum ghar me diya jalaayen kaise?

When the heart is full of darkness itself,

How should I illuminate my house?

Few minutes later.

Kool_Chandni: grrr8, awesome, mindboggling....i luv it yaar...u r gifted sir! n fyi I understood all of it!!

Aaftaab123: really...well haunsla-afzaai ka shukriya [thanks for the appreciation]

Kool_Chandni: u r welcome!

Aaftaab123: where?

Kool_Chandni: oh so u know how to flirt eh! Not bad Mr sun!

Dinkar types with a rarest of rare smile on his face while blushing at the same time.

Aaftaab123: if this is the case then you are the first victim of it.

Kool_Chandni: oh am honoured!....so Aaftaab is the pen name, u use in ur ghazals...now I get it! reminds me of someone just like you.

Dinkar doesn't ask who as he is scared that she might say it's her boyfriend.

Kool_Chandni: hey gotta go....time to go to bed...it was real pleasure chatting wid ya!

For the first time in his life, Dinkar feels the need to hold the time. He bids her adieu with an anonymous feeling in his heart.

Aaftaab123: same here...will I c u again?

Kool_Chandni: R u on facebook?

Aaftaab123: Nope

Kool_Chandni: do u skype?

Aaftaab123: Nope

Kool_Chandni: gr8! So you are still in early stages of evolution..lol!

Aaftaab123: I like it this way only. I am not a social being.

Kool_Chandni: jokes apart…I too prefer this way. Atleast I can imagine you the way I want. Tall, fair, handsome!

Aaftaab123: I am tall and fair [types Dinkar bashfully]

Kool_Chandni: I bet u r..k then.. 2morrow…same time, same place….cheerio!!

Aaftaab123: ciao.

Kool_Chandni: adeos!

Aaftaab123: Au revoir!

Kool_Chandni: dasvidaniya!

Aaftaab123: sayonara!

Kool_Chandni: enough is ….not enough…khuda hafiz. [lord is your protector]…he he!!

Aaftaab123: Allah hafiz! Gud nite n sweet dreamz. C ya tomorrow!!

Kool_Chandni logged out.

It is the maiden rendezvous with happiness for Dinkar, and so with the pangs of severance. The whole night Dinkar doesn't sleep and relives the moments spent with Chandni over and over, not because he never had warm, friendly confabulations with a girl before but because he never had them with anyone before.

Chapter 3

A Stint with Happiness

Dinkar wakes up late the next day and spends rest of the day writing a ghazal for his new-found friendship. The date sees a pleasant paradigm shift in the genre of his ghazal. They are no longer melancholic and sullen. Today the air is crisper and scented. The veils are drawn, and Dinkar's room sees sunlight after ages. The clock is ticking ever so slow, and the sun doesn't want to set as Dinkar eagerly waits to see Chandni online. He wants to empty his heart out today, which is otherwise headed for an emotional implosion.

It is 5 p.m. and Dinkar still has four hours to kill before his web-date. There's knocking on the door. Dinkar looks at his PC as if it were his messenger.

'Open the door, Dinkar.' It is his evil cousin Mayank. Dinkar opens the door reluctantly.

'I need to use your computer, bro! Mine is down with virus.' Mayank barges in and sticks his pen drive in the system without waiting for Dinkar's approval.

Mayank is tall and well-built, unlike Dinkar, who is emaciated, by his own choice, though similar in height.

Both of them are good-looking, but Dinkar has those sombre yet virtuous eyes with a seal of virgin all over his face while Mayank's face sweats impiety. He is like one of those studs whom you want to punch hard in the face without any viable reason every time you see them.

Though Dinkar is annoyed with Mayank's reprising visits, he chooses to defer reprisal.

'Your room has such a depressing aura,' shrills Mayank while running through his Facebook page.

'Ya, you forgot it here when you came in last time,' adds Dinkar, displaying his wits.

'Very funny! Okay, I am done.' He ejects out of Dinkar's room along with his pen drive.

After feeding the butterflies that were tickling his stomach the whole day, Dinkar takes position in front of his system, waiting for Chandni to come online. He doesn't need to wait much as she is quite punctual. There is again that rare blossom on Dinkar's face, which is becoming less rare now.

Aaftaab123: hiiiiiiiiiiiiiiiiiiiiiiiiiiiiiiii!!!!!!

Kool_Chandni: heyyyyyyyyyyyyyyyyyyyyyy!!!

Aaftaab123: how r u?

Kool_Chandni: better than you…ha ha ha!!

Aaftaab123: ofcourse you r…much better!!!

Kool_Chandni: really…thanx neways…n wassup?

Aaftaab123: fan

Kool_Chandni: its stale now…think something new!

Aaftaab123: ummmmmm…..sky?

Kool_Chandni: gud..atleast u came out of ur shell.

Aaftaab123: lol! Gud one!

[Though he doesn't laugh.]

Kool_Chandni: u juz typed it or u really laughed!!

Aaftaab123: how does it matter?

Kool_Chandni: juz tell me first?

Aaftaab123: juz typed it

Kool_Chandni: were u mocking at me?

Aaftaab123: no no…I really felt like laughing…plz don't get me wrong!

Kool_Chandni: then y didn't you?

Aaftaab123: I don't know…I never really laughed out loud as long as I remember.

Kool_Chandni: neva mind…your laughter drought is over…now you will laugh out loud…with me!!

Aaftaab123: am sure now I will…so how was ur day?

Kool_Chandni: grr8 as always, danced like hell!

Aaftaab123: really

Kool_Chandni: yep…it's my passion…life is a dance..dance is life!

Aaftaab123: for you…not for me!

Kool_Chandni: y?..u don't dance?

Aaftaab123: naah…not my cup of tea!

Kool_Chandni: u shud try..it's such a bliss.

Aaftaab123: I heard my mom was a good dancer.

Kool_Chandni: really! dats gr8. btw..wat happened to your parents?

Aaftaab123: they died in a terrorist attack.

Kool_Chandni: oh dear..so sorry to hear that…its really heartbreaking.

Aaftaab123: dats life for me.

Kool_Chandni: I wanna hug you tight rite now!

Dinkar gets goosebumps just by reading it.

Kool_Chandni: do u mind me asking where was this attack and when did it occur?

Aaftaab123: it was 29 october 2005…we had gone to Sarojini Nagar market. My parents were busy in pre diwali shopping when the blast took place.

Kool_Chandni: oh my god!...dats really terrible...that too on diwali eve! You still remember all that?

Aaftaab123: Nope, I don't.

Kool_Chandni: ohk..how did u survive?

Aaftaab123: I was told that just before the blast I ran off. my maid was saved too because of me.

Kool_Chandni: oh i c! I tell you these terrorists are bastards. What do they gain out of it?

Aaftaab123: curses from the ones suffering like me.

Kool_Chandni: u know how they r tricked into this?

Aaftaab123: how?

Kool_Chandni: they are promised a heavenly abode with 72 dark head virgins in after life.

Aaftaab123: what? r u serious?

Kool_Chandni: yes its true!!

Aaftaab123: heavenly abode for killing innocent people!! How can someone in his right senses fall for it?

Kool_Chandni: they do...millions of them!

Aaftaab123: I hope just one of them could come back and tell them, that they are befooled and misled.

Kool_Chandni: am sure someone, someday will!

Kool_Chandni: Lets chuck this topic now...temme...any new ghazal?

Aaftaab123: yep..fresh out of the oven!!

Kool_Chandni: oh..i din know u had to bake those after writing!

Aaftaab123: lol….n fyi this time I really laughed!

[Liar. He still didn't laugh!]

Kool_Chandni123: gud for u…to irshaad mere huzoor [recite, my sir]

Aaftaab123: ok..toh arz kiya hai [Here I begin]:

Kya bataaun ye kya tishnagi si hai,

Tu saath hai par teri kami si hai.

How do I explain this thirst,

I miss you while you are still with me.

Yun to basti ho tum meri saanson mein,

Dil phir bhi kahe ajnabi si hai.

You float in the air I breathe,

Still you are a stranger to the heart.

Kuchh hayaa hai teri, kuchh gairat meri,

Andaaz-e-mohabbat mein ik bebasi si hai.

It's your bashfulness and my modesty,

That we are not able to express love freely.

Sehar pe ikhtiyaar hai shab-e-suroor ka,

Aatish-e-'Aaftaab' mein ghuli 'Chandni' si hai.

The dawn is still intoxicated with glamour of night,

Such that the moonlight is dissolved in sunrays.

Jhaunka hawaa ka jo udaa gaya tera hijaab,

Thodi khushi hai thodi sharmindagi si hai.

When your veil came off with the gust of wind,

I felt happy and a bit embarrassed at the same time.

Main samandar hoon ek bejaan jazbaaton ka,

Tu behati aab-e-hayaat ki mujhme nadi si hai.

I am a dead sea of emotions,

And you flow into me like elixir of life.

Har waqt labon par dua ke tera deedar ho,

Ab samjhaa kyun mohabbat bandagi si hai.

I am always praying to catch one glimpse of yours,

Now I realize why loving someone is like worshipping.

Tu pehli nahin hai jispe fidaa hua 'Aaftaab',

Tu lagti magar mujhe aakhiri si hai.

You are not the first one whom 'Aaftaab' has fallen for,

But you are certainly the last one.

Few moments later.

Kool_Chandni: Subhan Allah!! [Glorious is God.] I don hav words Dinkar!! Fantabulous!! Whoa!!

Aaftaab123: Nazar-e-karam farmaane ka shukriya!! [Thanks for showering your grace]

Kool_Chandni: Especially the 4th couplet...thanx 4 inserting my name in there...am honoured... Aata hai mera naam jab bhi tere naam ke saath, jaane kyun log mere naam se jal jaate hain! Ha ha ha.. [Whenever my name is taken along with yours, why do people envy my name?]

Aaftaab123: Waah waah waah...ye umr aur ye soch... [Great! Such deep thoughts in this tender age.]

Dinkar types playfully.

Kool_Chandni: learnt from u only sir..but really Dinkar... thats amazing transition in one day...so no more sad poetry now...okay?

Aaftaab123: okay!!...deal! if you agree to be mine forever.

That's what Dinkar wanted to write but, without a second thought, presses Backspace and retypes.

Aaftaab123: okay!!...deal! if you agree to be my friend forever.

Kool_Chandni: deal!! Friends Forever!!

Aaftaab123: hey..do u hav a pic?

Kool_Chandni: yep...I do!

Aaftaab123: may I c?

Kool_Chandni: ye kali, jab talak phool bankar khile, intezaar...intezaar...intezaar karo! [Wait until this bud becomes a flower. Chandni recites an old movie song!]

Aaftaab123: Waah waah!...ye umr aur ye soch! [Great. Such deep thoughts in this tender age.]

Kool_Chandni: ha ha ha!...I'll show u soon dear! Hey, gimme ur mobile no. we'll whatsapp.

Aaftaab123: I don't have one.

Kool_Chandni: then how many u have...ha ha ha

Aaftaab123: very funny

Kool_Chandni: Who on earth doesn't have fone now a days? Even beggars beg via fone!

Aaftaab123: lol..but I never felt the need. I don't even have landline in my room!

Kool_Chandni: u really r a loner! Now gotta go!

Aaftaab123: okay, I'll get one soon! Please don't get mad at me!

Kool_Chandni: ha ha ha! No dear, I really need to go. Am not mad at u.

Aaftaab123: infact was waiting whole day to chat wid you!!

Kool_Chandni: oh shooo shweeeet...now wait again until day after tomorrow...!

Aaftaab123: You won't be comin 2morrow?

It is heartbreaking for Dinkar to learn that he will not be able to meet her tomorrow.

Kool_Chandni: no..hav a function to attend!

Aaftaab123: ohk!! C ya then…day after!

Kool_Chandni: bubye..shabba khair! [good night]

Aaftaab123: bye..shabba khair…take care!

Kool_Chandni: u2

Kool_Chandni logged out.

Dinkar keeps staring at the screen for a while, hoping to hear a *knock knock* again in the messenger from Chandni, but it was not to be. Finally, with hands that seem reluctant to obey his command at first, he has his way and switches off the system and turns off the lights. The room is filled with moonlight as soon as the lights go off. Today his room, as well as his heart, is shimmering with *chandni*. He lies in bed and paints her picture on the canvas of his mind. He paints her a beautiful face like that of a Bollywood actress that hasn't gone under the knife. He gives her long black hair that float in air even without the wind. He gives her a perfect curvy body with ample bosoms. Her voice is so sweet and melodious that everything she says sounds like a Beethoven's symphony to his ears. He places himself next to her and begins to palaver with her, cuddle with her, feels her warm scented breath against his face, unravels her silky hair as he recites his ghazals. Dinkar has undergone renaissance.

And as is the tradition, this infatuation relieves Dinkar of his duty to sleep at night. All the joy in his heart makes him a little unnerved as he is not used to it. The other thing that baffles him is as to how long this stint with happiness would last. His mind is doing the math while his heart is in trepidation. He is Hindu; she is Muslim. What is the future of this relationship? He gets up and finds his pen and notepad to write a couplet he just conceived.

Yun to ishq ki hoti koi zaat nahin,

Ho sakta ye hamara umr bhar ka saath nahin.

Love doesn't have any caste or religion,

Yet I think our relation won't last lifelong.

Tu Eid ka chaand, main Diwali ka diya,

Chaand ke naseeb mein bhi Diwali ki raat nahin.

You are moon of Eid, am an oil lamp of Diwali,

Hence moon will always be bereft of Diwali [as it's a no moon night].

He wants to have a contingency plan ready in case Chandni leaves him in distress. But again, he has the master plan— i.e. to end it all.

'Oh, you poor thing. I don't know how to please you.' That's what God must be saying to Dinkar. But Dinkar is pessimism personified, incapable of perceiving the good or, in devil' s theology, a genius in extracting the dejection out of nowhere, no matter how blissful the situation may be.

Sometimes I think how cool it would be if there were some kind of magic soap that could cleanse our aura and wash off all the negativity from our mind and soul as soon as we shower. It'll be the most expensive soap without a doubt.

Chapter 4

The Plagiarist Cousin

Dinkar suddenly wakes up in the middle of the night, sweating like a cold drink bottle. He again had that recurring nightmare that has haunted him throughout his life. He saw a man standing with a turban who had wrapped his face by the extra strip of cloth hanging from his headgear so that only his eyes were visible. His upper body was wrapped in a blanket, and he carried a Kalashnikov in one hand. He had intense eyes that tried to convey a message which Dinkar has always failed to decipher. Then he removed the blanket, and it fell to the ground. The blanket was hiding the suicide vest he was wearing. In a matter of seconds, he pressed the trigger that was tied to his wrist and blew himself up.

Dinkar wipes the sweat off his face and gulps some water. He lowers the temperature of air conditioner by a couple of degrees and goes back to sleep.

The good thing about nightmares is that they make us realize how wonderful the reality is. But Dinkar is one hard nut to crack.

The next day, Dinkar spends in daydreaming in the kingdom of Dinkarpur, where he is the emperor and Chandni, his only queen, and he has no harem full of mistresses. He builds her a Chand Mahal (an upgrade over the Taj Mahal, with a revolving dome and a telescope to see the moon) while she is still alive. He loses one leg in the great battle against the British that results in their ouster after which he comes to be known as Dinkar the Lame the Great. Mayank is beheaded in front of the crowd, accused of slander against the king while the uncle and aunt are exiled to the Himalayas. But these heroics are just limited to his dreams. In reality, the guy is even scared to step on the roof.

Today Dinkar has to make a daring endeavour as Chandni wasn't coming online and sleep was nowhere on the horizon, plausibly due to the antidepressants he was taking. After his dinner, he somehow gathers courage, holds his nerves and marches on to the terrace while his lean legs still tremble. Ever since he was little, he had never been on the terrace after dark or even during the daytime because the monkey-man would come and scathe him with his steel claws who once used to hound people sleeping on the roofs in Delhi as the folklore suggests.

It's a breezy night with just the right temperatures and faint moonlight and negligible mosquito activity. As he arrives on the terrace, an estranged gust meets him as if enquiring his business here. He leans on the railings gazing at the space, unaware of the fact that a damsel on the adjacent terrace gazes at him.

'Hey!' she yells from her terrace. Dinkar gets alarmed and runs towards the stairs, apprehending the arrival of monkey-man. But soon he realizes that he pre-empted falsely while the girl discovers she has a scary side too. Dinkar makes an embarrassed walk back to his spot like a batsman returning to pavilion after being bowled out on duck. He says hello in an inaudible voice, avoiding any eye contact.

'What happened, dude? Why did you run away? Did I scare you?' the girl asks curiously.

Dinkar raises his head and takes a good look at her. She is a beautiful, fair, teenage girl in her pink night dress clad in a black stole. Her long black silky straight hair floats in the air with the wind and disappear in the backdrop of night sky. Even Dinkar finds it hard to take his eyes off her. Is it his new-found interest in girls, or is she something else? The truth is she resembles the image of Chandni he had created in his mind. It is like the heavens have answered his prayers and Chandni's apparition is telepathically transferred in front of him. She has become his dream girl at first sight.

'No, no, nothing like that. I thought someone was calling me from below,' Dinkar manages to subvert the topic.

'Oh, I see! So you are Mayank's cousin?' asks the girl.

'Yes, I am. My name is Dinkar. How do you know Mayank?' Dinkar enquires.

'I am Jahanvi, and I study in the same college as Mayank. We are friends, you know!' replies Jahanvi cheerfully.

'So where are you from, and when did you arrive here?' asks Jahanvi.

First embarrassing moment. 'No, no. I live here only, on the first floor,' tells Dinkar while looking down, realizing what he had lost all this while, having been confined to his room.

'You must be kidding, dude, coz I have never seen you before since we moved in last year,' exclaims Jahanvi.

It is becoming more and more tormenting to explain for Dinkar, but he has to. 'I go to sleep early, maybe that's why!'

'What about daytime?' pokes Jahanvi.

'Well, I ... I don't step out much,' blurts Dinkar.

'Oh, I see! But how come Mayank never told me about you?' she asks.

'That you should ask Mayank.' Dinkar shrugs.

'I'll surely do. So which college are you in?' asks Jahanvi.

Second embarrassing moment.

'I left after passing [failing] high school.' babbles Dinkar.

'Really, no more studies. That is so cool. My parents won't budge. You are one lucky bastard.' Jahanvi chuckles.

Dinkar feels so light after hearing that. Not bastard but the fact that Jahanvi didn't frown upon him due to academic falling. He falls in love again, twice in two days.

'So, dude, what else do you do besides shying away from the world?' asks Jahanvi.

'I am a poet,' says Dinkar confidently as he had discovered lately that it works with girls.

'Really! So both of you have the same talent!' says Jahanvi vibrantly.

'What do you mean by both?' asks Dinkar as lines on his forehead deepen.

'Mayank too writes ghazals, no! Though I don't get them, but he says he writes for me! Cool no, dude?' tells Jahanvi proudly with a big smile.

'Do you remember any of his ghazals?' asks bewildered Dinkar, faking a smile.

'Ya, yesterday only he recited one! Khandharon me something something dhoondte hain,' informs Jahanvi.

'What!' cries Dinkar, wiping off the smile from his face as he feels robbed. 'And he told you he had written it?'

'Ya, dude, *for me*,' says Jahanvi, emphasizing on 'for me'.

'How can he write that for you? It's so depressing. Did you even get a word of it?' asks Dinkar, irritated by her ignorance and of constantly being addressed dude. Ignorance sure is bliss, more like a bomb wrapped as bliss waiting to explode when fired with correct information. 'He didn't write it in the first place. I wrote it. Oh, so that's why he keeps barging into my room on pretext of using my computer,' shrieks Dinkar as he connects the dots and accuses Mayank of plagiarism.

'Son of a bitch. He told me he wrote it *for me*,' fumes Jahanvi, once again highlighting 'for me'. 'Let that pig come!'

They don't have to wait long, thus providing crucial circumstantial evidence to the theory of 'Think of the devil and the devil is here'.

'Well, well, well, it seems somebody forgot the way to his cell. Wind is too strong. Hold the railings tight, bro,' says Mayank histrionically with a nefarious face hinting at Dinkar's lean body.

'Hello, my love,' he greets Jahanvi.

'Hello, my ass!' greets back Jahanvi while signalling her displeasure as she flips the bird.

'How dare you steal my ghazals,' Dinkar grabs Mayank by his collar before he could react to Jahanvi's gesture.

'Bro! Let it go if you don't wanna lose your teeth!' threatens Mayank.

'Don't you dare enter my room again,' says Dinkar as he lets go of his collar.

'What you did to him is bad, but what you did to me is really sick,' starts Jahanvi. 'You said you wrote those ghazals *for me*, and now he tells me he wrote them, not you, and that it's all sad stuff. I would have made a fool of myself had I posted it on Facebook. How could you do that to me, Mayank? All you guys are the same. You just want sex, and you'll go to any extent for that,' prattles Jahanvi inexorably as Mayank struggles to find a stop button on this one.

Did she say sex? thinks Dinkar to himself. Mayank and Jahanvi are having sex! He could not believe his ears. Did he hear *six* or *sex*. While the former made no sense, it must be *sex*.

The wild scenes of Mayank and Jahanvi making love while Mayank recites Dinkar's ghazals begin to hover in front of his eyes. He forgets about the ensuing brawl between Mayank and Jahanvi, and now only one thing plays on his mind: Mayank had sex with this girl, this gorgeous girl, whom he is afraid to touch lest he blemishes her, this sweet-scented goddess, this dream girl, although a dumb one. How could he? How could he be so lucky? Now he hates him even more, the more he thinks about it. The crime of laying hands on his ghazal mitigates in front of the crime of laying hands on his dream girl.

When the emotional dust settles, he finds himself on his own on the terrace. He feels betrayed, mugged, and demoralized. And as if his pique is communicated to the tectonic plates below, mild tremors rock the city as people rush out of their homes except Dinkar, who returns to his room. He takes a sleeping pill and dozes off.

Chapter 5

It's Payback Time

The next evening, Dinkar awaits eagerly for Chandni to come online. Hours pass by, but she doesn't turn up. He goes through the news meanwhile in order to keep his knowledge current. The top news story is about the earthquake that hit northern India yesterday night though the epicentre was in Pakistan where it did bulk of damage with about two hundred casualties while in India, only cracks appeared in some old buildings as the ripples were diminished in intensity.

Dinkar is remorseful because he feels he has been disloyal to Chandni as he was enchanted by Jahanvi, though that affair could not stretch beyond a few minutes. But nevertheless he has found another reason to be compunctious, and it paves a way for another ghazal.

Ye aag nigaahon ne lagaai hogi,

Koi aah aankhon tak aayi hogi.

The eyes must have started this fire,

A sigh must have reached the eye.

Kyun muqammal vo kabhi hanste nahin,

Koi hasrat dil me dabaai hogi.

Why doesn't she laugh open-heartedly?

An unfilled desire must be buried in her heart.

Is safar se kuchh haasil na hoga,

Tanhaaiyon ke aage bhi tanhaai hogi.

No good can come out of this journey,

There will be more desolation after desolation.

Jaan atki hai aaj haashiye pe,

Usne phir meri kasam uthaai hogi.

Life again hangs by a thin string,

She must have sworn by me.

Raha hoga zaroor vo tujhse khafa,

Ye tasveer teri jisne banaai hogi.

He must have been annoyed with you.

The one who made this painting of yours.

Kar sakta khuda ye galati nahin,

Mohabbat insaan ne hi banaai hogi.

God cannot commit this blunder,

Love must have been invented by humans.

Jee raha hai ajab khushfehmi me 'Aaftaab',

Koi yaad karta hai jo chheenk aayi hogi.

'Aaftaab' is living in a false optimism,

He thinks someone misses him if he sneezes.

Days pass by like millennia as Dinkar relentlessly awaits Chandni to return online, stationed in front of his computer sans sleep, shower, and hope until his aunt intervenes.

'Open the door, Dinkar. Oh my god, your room is stinking,' says Aunt while shrinking her nose.

As Dinkar opens the door, Aunt is jolted as if she has seen a zombie. Dinkar stands there with big dark spots under his eyes like a commando on a search-and-rescue mission and hair pointing like antennae as if scanning the location of Chandni.

'Hey bhagwaan [oh lord], I just went out for few days and look, what have you made of yourself. Go take a shower now while I get your room cleaned,' orders Aunt.

Dinkar's room resembles the cabin of a vessel caught in a storm. Aunt tiptoes through the room in order to avoid stepping on the stuff scattered around. There is the leftover food and plates which came in but never found a way out as the maid was too scared to confront Dinkar.

Dinkar quietly slips into the bathroom.

'Get ready fast, we have to go visit Dr Malhotra,' tells Aunt in a strident voice. Dr Malhotra is Dinkar's latest psychiatrist.

'Nandiniiii . . . he is in the bathroom. You can come up and clean his room,' hollers Aunt to the maid.

Nandini is in her early thirties, but she looks much younger. She is like one of those naturally bosomy women who wear unnaturally wide and deep neck suits and blouses flaunting their cleavages to the deprived and the desperate. She is from a small village in Uttar Pradesh. Her husband died five years ago, leaving her issueless. For the past three years, she has been with the Chauhan family as a full-time maid.

Thirty minutes later, Dinkar emerges out of the bathroom, fresh and sterile. 'I am not going anywhere near that psycho psychiatrist. He drives me crazy,' screams Dinkar as he petrifies Nandini to drop the plates she is holding.

'Gosh! Why are you scaring the girl?' cries Aunt. 'And why are you so scared of him? Go down and clean it later,' tells exasperated Aunt and Nandini runs down for cover as if her life was in danger.

Nandini isn't scared of Dinkar for no reason. Last year she got violently thrashed on to a wall by Dinkar. Yes, it's true, though Dinkar is not a violent person at all.

It was the same day when Dinkar screwed up his suicide. One fine morning, as Nandini entered Dinkar's room for cleaning, she saw Dinkar crying like a baby, holding a paper in his hand. She asked Dinkar as to why he was crying and held him in her arms. Dinkar thought he could use a shoulder too. It is then that she tried to siphon some pleasure and started kissing Dinkar. Realizing that he was being molested, Dinkar pushed her against the wall and ran towards the balcony and jumped. Nandini just suffered a bump in her head though that incident gave her a phobia of Dinkar. Neither she nor Dinkar told anyone about it.

'Now what's wrong with Dr Malhotra?' asks already frustrated Aunt.

'He has a big mole under his nostril and whistles as he speaks. It's so agonizing to talk to him,' complains Dinkar.

'You have problems with all of them. The last one blinked too much, so you got him changed. How many doctors are we going to change? How else are you going to get better?' asks Aunt, stymied by his pig-headedness.

'Nothing is wrong with me. I am fine. And I have decided. From now on, I'll live life on the edge. I want to try everything before I die,' says Dinkar resolutely.

Aunt's plastered face begins to lose lustre as she asks in a shaky voice, 'Are you going to commit suicide again?'

That day when Nandini tried to rape Dinkar, he had flunked his class 10 board exams. He jumped from his balcony only to land on his uncle who, at the time, was sitting in the courtyard, enjoying his daily dose of horoscopes, while reading a newspaper, which read 'Trouble befalls you today starting now!' Poor guy got a fractured arm and slipped disc while Dinkar walked without a scratch, only twisting his ankle. So now you can fathom Aunt's concern.

'Chill, Auntie, it's just an expression of speech. I won't commit suicide,' consoles Dinkar. Aunt takes a sigh of relief before Dinkar drops another bomb. 'I am going to have sex!'

'What!' cries Aunt while on the verge of a cardiac arrest. 'What did you say?'

'You heard it right. I am going to a prostitute to have sex,' proclaims Dinkar as if it just came to him in epiphany.

Aunt is stunned by the blatant wish expressed by Dinkar but gathers herself and sermonizes, 'Beta [Son], this is not the age to do all these things. What is—'

'If Mayank can do it, why can't I?' Dinkar cuts her short.

Lightning strikes the Aunt this time, like defibrillation after cardiac arrest.

She asks wailing, 'Why did Mayank have sex . . . when . . . with whom?'

'With Jahanvi, our neighbour,' informs Dinkar.

'Haye ram [oh, Lord Ram], with Pammi's daughter? Wahi chudail mili thi use? [He found that witch only?]' sobs Aunt.

'No, Auntie, she is gorgeous,' muses Dinkar.

'Shut up! I am talking about Pammi. Where is this Mayank? Call him up now!' roars Auntie.

It was payback time for Mayank. With utmost pleasure, Dinkar jumps down the stairs to inform Mayank of the checkmate.

'Dude, you are screwed!' Dinkar informs Mayank while having a treacherous laugh that would have even belittled Raavan.

'Nothing, it's just my cousin. He is a bit retarded you know! Okay, I'll call ya later. Bye. Love you. Mmmuaahh!' Mayank disconnects the call while turning his attention to Dinkar. 'What is wrong with you?' shouts Mayank.

'I told Auntie that you had sex.' Dinkar laughs again.

'What! You are kidding right?' Mayank panics while Dinkar performs a poorly choreographed dance.

'We . . . we were not having sex, she was . . . she was just cleaning my room!' stutters Mayank.

'Who was cleaning the room?' asks Dinkar, astounded by the new piece of information.

'Whom did you tell Mom I was having sex with?' freaks Mayank.

'Oh my god, oh my god. This is big,' says Dinkar as he runs towards the stairs while Mayank follows suit.

'Dinkar, stop . . . Dinkar, please . . . Dinkar, don't mess with me, Dinkar,' warns Mayank while his heart pounds heavily, but it is too late. Dinkar is already at the doorstep where his aunt is sitting with her head between her hands.

'Auntie, he is doing Nandini too!' breaks Dinkar fervently while grasping for breath.

Aunt looks at Dinkar in horror, then drops on the floor.

'Mom, I swear I didn't do anything.' Mayank arrives, pushing aside Dinkar. He is appalled to see his mother lying on the floor.

'What are you looking at, you idiot? Help me pick her up,' Mayank calls for Dinkar's assistance.

They both shake her up and help her to the chair while Mayank fetches a bottle of water.

'Are you okay, Mom?' asks Mayank as she gulps in some water.

While her eyes are still half-closed, she asks Mayank in an incoherent drunkard's parlance, 'Did you . . . did you?'

'No, Mom, I didn't. I swear.' Mayank doesn't allow her to finish.

'Did you use protection?' asks Aunt.

'No, Mom, I didn't—what?' realizing he answered that one real quick.

'I don't want to be a grandma so soon,' says Aunt while still coming to her senses.

'Auntie, you forgot about the AIDS and syphilis,' goes Dinkar again, leaving no opportunity of extracting gratification out of the situation.

'I didn't do anything, Mom. Dinkar is just making it up. Don't believe him,' pleads Mayank.

'Oh yeah! Why don't we take him for a virginity test then?' Dinkar chuckles.

'There's no virginity test for men, you moron,' informs Mayank.

'There is.'

'Is not.'

'There is.'

'Shut up, boys! My head is going to explode,' yells aunt. 'Let your father come, then we will decide what to do with you,' Aunt intimidates Mayank, 'and I'll fire that bitch, now.'

'But, Mom, why don't you believe me? Please don't tell Papa,' whines Mayank as he tries to persuade her.

'Not a word from you now, Mayank. Go to your room!' orders Aunt as she proceeds to terminate the services of the maid, thus forgetting about the wish Dinkar had made earlier, from where it all began. Mayank too retires to his room, cursing Dinkar all the way and beyond.

Chapter 6

Sex and the City

Dinkar sneaks out of the gate and looks for an auto (as the motorized three-wheeler rickshaws are fondly called here) to discover the new realms of manhood.

'Bhaiya GB road chaloge?' [Will you go to GB road, brother?] Dinkar asks an autorickshaw driver. The driver turns his head to the side, signalling sit down. GB road is a red light district in Delhi.

'Going to see someone?' asks the driver as the auto gains speed.

'No, just going to have sex,' replies Dinkar, leaning back.

'Nobody goes there to meditate!' says the driver, while bursting into a weird laughter, honking in resonance, then offering Dinkar a high five, which returns unattended.

'Osho said it's like meditation only,' argues Dinkar.

'Who is Ashu? Your brother? I too have one brother named Ashu. He is blah blah blah . . .' jabbers the driver, looking in the rear view, whose talking speed as well as volume is directly proportional to the speed of his autorickshaw. The more he accelerates, the faster and louder he speaks.

'Not Ashu, Osho! Forget it! Just drive,' tells Dinkar annoyingly.

'So this is your first time?' asks the driver.

Dinkar just nods his head in agreement.

'My first time was with my wife,' tells the driver vivaciously. 'How old are you?'

'Sixteen,' replies Dinkar devoid of interest.

'I was only fourteen then,' says the driver with a sense of achievement.

'You got married when you were fourteen?' asks Dinkar with revival of interest.

'Nai, saab . . . shaadi to hamari 7 saal me hi ho gayi thi . . . gona hamara 14 mein hua tha [No, sir . . . I got married when I was seven, but I brought her home when I was fourteen]', tells driver filled with nostalgia as the auto slows down and halts and the driver goes silent as if he was connected to the engines too.

It seems like a jam, which are a common sight in Delhi. There is freedom of speech, press, religion, expression, corruption, but there is still no freedom of movement here. Once on the road, you are at the mercy of religious gatherings, political rallies, convoys, remonstrant blockades, and marriage processions. Marriages are made in heaven, celebrated on earth, and blown out of proportions in India. Soon a whole industry of vendors emerges out of nowhere as the jam is a godsend to them. They sell toys, pirated books, car window shades, drinks, and eatables. Some clean the already shining cars voluntarily as they appear to be social workers but later demand money for their service. Then there are others who just sell good wishes and ask money in the name of God.

An hour later, Dinkar finally arrives at his destination with the auto-biographer-driver.

'How much?' asks Dinkar.

'250, sir,' says the driver, expecting to renegotiate, but Dinkar hands him over a 500 rupee note.

'All the best, sir. Fateh karo [Be victorious],' wishes the driver, handing him back the balance as Dinkar sets foot on GB road to lay a sexual siege.

As Dinkar steps out of the auto, he finds himself in a labyrinth, perturbed to see so many people jostling around. He looks around the shabby antiquated houses with women of all age and size posing in their balconies, inviting and teasing any and every passer-by who appears to be a potential customer.

In order to escape the mayhem, Dinkar enters the first brothel on his side. He climbs up the uneven stairs and enters the salon. He sees five women seated there in fancy multicoloured blouses and petticoats gleaming like a colourful oil sheen over the polluted waters. They wear loud make-up similar to that of Dinkar's aunt, and none of them appear attractive by his standards. Nevertheless, their eyes light up to see a customer as they chuckle gleefully.

The brothel chaperon, or Auntie as some call her, halts Dinkar as he starts to make a U-turn. 'I have young girls too, come have a seat!'

Dinkar nervously takes a seat on the edge of the sofa with the three other women.

'First time?' asks one of them.

Dinkar blushes away as he nods. All the ladies tease him and take turn in plucking his already reddened cheeks as if it was some sort of cult ritual that they have to perform every time a virgin customer arrives.

'Aa rahi hai teri item [Your girl is on the way],' informs one of the inmates.

Auntie escorts one comparatively younger-looking girl and a better-looking one too and for a change, she is wearing an eye-soothing off-white ghagra choli [long skirt-blouse]

'I'll charge 1,000 for her. You like her?' asks Auntie.

Dinkar, left with no other option, succumbs to the pressures of virility and agrees to abide by the terms.

'Mujra kab shuru hoga? [When will the dance performance begin?]' asks Dinkar with excitement.

All the inmates erupt in unison.

'Mujraa', and all laugh even louder while an embarrassed Dinkar analyses his words again.

'Kahan se aaye ho nawabzaade? [Where do you hail from, son of Nawab?]' asks one of the girls while they all struggle to control the laugh riot.

Mujra is an outdated tradition of the brothels where they used to have dance and booze with meaningful lyrics and classical Indian music played by musicians alongside, or at least that's what Bollywood movies portray. Dinkar's assumption was too based on them. We all make assumptions, from time to time, that fail miserably in the light of truth. For instance, when I was young, I assumed that lesbians hail from a country called Lesbia.

'There will be no mujra-vujra here. Take her inside the room and get about your business, but pay first,' directs Auntie as the tranquillity sets in the house.

After paying the money, Dinkar drearily follows the girl to the room, as his enthusiasm is trimmed with no prospects of mujra taking place.

'And listen, be gentle,' bellows Auntie as she issues a last-minute decree.

While at home, Mayank is busy going through Dinkar's stuff in order to sabotage him so that he can set the scoreboards even. Dinkar left in a jiffy and forgot to lock his room. Now it lies at Mayank's mercy. He hears a *knock knock* on Dinkar's messenger. He checks, and it's Kool_Chandni online.

Kool_Chandni: hiiiiiiiiiiii!!!!!

Aaftaab123: hey sexy!

Kool_Chandni: Is it Dinkar?

Aaftaab123: No, it's his cousin Mayank.

Kool_Chandni: so I thought, couldn't be Dinkar.

Aaftaab123: Ya…he is so boring na!

Kool_Chandni: No, not at all. Infact he is the most interesting guy I have met yet and talented too. u don't know ur bro much, do ya?

Aaftaab123: Its time u shud know abt him. He is wid a prostitute as we chat.

Kool_Chandni: whattt?..no ways…can't be! u r lying. Not Dinkar.

Aaftaab123: He goes every week. Ask for urself when he comes back.

Kool_Chandni: I will…tell him I'll be waiting for him until midnight.

Aaftaab123: Okay will do…Btw…r u interested in sex chat?

Kool_Chandni: nice talking to u pervert…bye!

Kool_Chandni logged out.

Chandni goes invisible on Mayank's invitation while it isn't the first time for Mayank as he is used to such commemoration from girls. Inferring mission accomplished,

Mayank lays everything in erstwhile position and leaves the room in jubilation.

Dinkar and his girl enter a petite room, not the cleanest but cleaner than Dinkar's, although it's old and crumbling with plaster tapering off, thus exposing the bricks intermittently, while Dinkar has unsolicited audience for his live sex show in the form of lizards crawling over the walls. There is a single bed and a small table on the side with a fan and an old cassette player atop, and that concludes our inventory of the room.

The girl lights a bidi and asks Dinkar to strip as she slips two condoms out of her blouse and on the table. These downmarket prostitutes in India seldom strive for customer satisfaction. They will be either busy changing audio cassettes in the player or munching peanuts while you are doing them, as if refusing to acknowledge your existence, thus making them less accountable in case it's a sin. But this wasn't the case with Dinkar as she knew it's his first time.

'You come here and lie down, I will do it,' tells the girl.

Dinkar obeys like a well-bred boy and lies on the bed face down.

'I am not going to give you a massage. Lie on your back,' tells the vexed girl.

Dinkar embarrassingly turns around and lies on his back.

The sex education in Indian schools is to be blamed for, which is non-existent as it's still a taboo to talk about sex in this country whose population is ever proliferating like an epidemic. Until I was fourteen, I used to think that women get pregnant by virtue of the magical powers of wedding garlands, or *varmala*, and vedic hymns chanted during the marriage ceremony.

The girl lifts her ghagra and hikes over Dinkar as they resemble a small sailboat docked alongside a wharf. She gently rubs against him as Dinkar gets ticklish.

'What's your name?' asks Dinkar.

'Bipasa basu,' girl giggles while biting her lower lip.

'It's Bipasha, not Bipasa,' corrects Dinkar as she massages his chest.

'What's yours?' asks the girl.

'John Abraham,' says Dinkar skilfully as the girl sets off in frenzy.

'Oh John . . . ohhhh, John,' girl moans ersatz.

'So where are you from?' asks Dinkar.

'Enough of talking already. Now get it erect! I don't have all night,' tells the enraged girl.

'I don't know how to do that. Normally it gets on its own,' informs worried Dinkar. 'I think it'll help if you take off your clothes,' suggests Dinkar though it was a bad advice.

The girl obliges as she takes off her blouse. Instead of getting an arousal, Dinkar begins to feel squeamish at the sight of her armpit hair and odour. She tries to stimulate Dinkar, kisses him passionately as he somehow controls not to puke. She pulls out all the tricks from the book, but it won't budge. After three minutes, Dinkar finally surrenders and ejaculates vomit on her face as she is closing in to kiss him. The condoms on the table take a sigh of relief as they saved face today. Speaking of condoms, you know what will be a catchy line for a condom campaign? 'No tissues, no issues!'

While on the wall, the guest lizard asks the host lizard, 'Is that what you invited me for? What a lousy show they put on. Come over to my room tomorrow, and I'll show you some real homo sapiens sex, baby!'

The girl howls like crazy as she storms out of the room, blinded by the vomit without realizing she was half-naked. All the other women and a few customers in the gallery are awestruck to see her face and the rest. The chaperone comes to her rescue and quickly recedes with her in the adjacent room.

Dinkar hurriedly gets into his clothes and slips out of the room, thence down the stairs exploiting the attention deficit created by the ruckus. Once on the street, he dashes for a few hundred metres, fearing being chased. On gaining safe distance, he halts, once rest assured of no trails.

He notices two young girls as they chortle while staring at Dinkar. Dinkar is fair, tall, and handsome, and he ought to receive such adulation from girls though his lean body plays a spoilsport. His feelings of grandiose soon subside as he realizes that the girls are ogling at the protrusion in his pants. Oh dear, now it rises! Well, better late than never.

Finally, he got the blood flowing in his loins. He turns back, forth, back, and forth unable to decide which way to head. While going back to the same place was out of the question, there is a whole buffet of them, although there is no surety that his better half-inch will not prank upon him again. He decides to adjourn the quest and decides to go back home.

As he looks for an auto, a restaurant-cum-bar attracts his attention across the road. In order to turn his misadventure into an escapade, he decides to try alcohol for the first time and also satisfy his craving for meat simultaneously. He enters the apparently sordid place, and it's dim inside. He chooses a table in a relatively empty corner of the bar, away from other men enjoying their drinks. A waiter quickly presents him with the menu. He scans the menu and orders the most expensive peg of whisky available though it is still not a scotch. He had read somewhere that if you must drink, drink a good quality alcohol as it will do less harm. Waiter asks him whether he will have it in water, soda, or cold drink. He says water as he wants to relish its real taste because he is under a misconception that people drink alcohol for its taste. He orders mutton seekh kabab alongside the drink. No one cares to check his ID or age, and he is served his drink promptly with complimentary peanuts while he has to wait for the kababs to be grilled. Four ice cubes float in the golden brown liquid resembling honey syrup in a hexagonal glass kept in front of him on a round table. The juices in his mouth inundate his tongue in anticipation of tasting something majestic like an elixir. He grabs the glass and takes a teensy sip so that he doesn't finish it quickly as he wants to savour it for a long time. As soon as he learns its pungent taste, he spits it back in the glass, more than he sipped with his wrinkled nose and diminished eyes. He suspects that the waiter must have served something else in the name of whisky. This cannot be its real taste as he has seen many relatives drooling just on hearing about the prospects of whisky being served in a function they are invited to. He immediately calls the waiter.

'This tastes funny and has a foul smell. Must be stale,' tells Dinkar. The waiter looks at him flummoxed, not sure if Dinkar was serious or just playing a prank on him.

'Is it your first time?' he asks.

'Yes,' says Dinkar.

'Whisky tastes like this only!' says the waiter.

'Really? If it smells and tastes so bad, why do people drink it?' asks Dinkar.

'Ha ha ha,' laughs the waiter. 'It's not the taste. It's the after-effect that they drink for. If you want taste, drink single malt scotch,' says the waiter. Though the single malt too would appear bitter for a beginner. 'Try it in a soft drink,' suggests the waiter.

Dinkar agrees. He dilutes it further with cola. The new taste is somewhat acceptable, but he still struggles to force it down his throat. His kababs arrive too. Thankfully, the kababs taste heavenly. As more and more alcohol sinks in his body and mind, the inanimate things begin to come to life. The ice cubes flip in the whisky like dolphins in the golden sea. The glass skates on the coaster around the table like a ballerina on ice. Everything around him seems to dance as he hums a tune. After a few more sips, his head begins to feel a little heavy and eyes dizzy. He asks for the bill as he fears he might fall asleep here. The waiter presents the inflated bill with taxes more than the product itself. Dinkar pays the bill without checking. He walks out like a child taking his first steps. Soon he manages to grab an auto back home. The wind blows his inebriation away to some extent during the ride. After thirty minutes, he reaches home, unchaste but virgin.

Chapter 7

A Place Far, Far Away

Inside the house, the countdown has begun, and Uncle is already on ignition mode fuelled by his fury, supported by the payload of Aunt. The launch signal comes in the form of screeching of iron gates as Dinkar enters the premises.

'Don't you dare enter this house,' fumes Uncle as he confronts Dinkar.

'It's my house, not yours!' roars Dinkar even louder while Uncle is dumbfounded as he witnesses another dimension of Dinkar. It is the whisky in him doing the talking. Nevertheless, Aunt furnishes some decibels in favour of her hubby, 'How dare you speak to your uncle in a raised voice? Even I never did that!'

And Uncle goes in his mind, *Oh, really?*

'Please leave me alone, and don't interfere in my life,' petitions Dinkar.

'So that you can go to prostitutes and might as well bring them home one day, you rascal,' goes Uncle again, rejuvenated by the brief silence.

'Yes, I will do whatever I want. It's my life and my house. I can bring prostitutes and have sex whenever I want!' howls Dinkar again as neighbours begin to peep through their windows. Uncle completely loses it this time as he raises his hand to thrash Dinkar.

'If Mayank can do it, why can't I?' screams Dinkar while covering his face with both arms. He keys in the correct password with just a few seconds to spare to abort the attack. Uncle doesn't have the answer to Dinkar's question and is thus forced to retract his hand.

Aunt tries to pacify Uncle as she signals Dinkar to retire to his room with her eyes.

Dinkar promptly heads to his room, thus escaping the quandary.

'Where is this Mayank? I want to see that bastard right now! Mayank!' hollers Uncle enraged.

'Why are you calling him bastard, ji[1]? He is your own son!' reminds Aunt.

'Shut up, Pushpa!'

'I swear, he is your son,' compels Auntie.

'Offo . . . I know he is my son,' says Uncle while scratching his barren scalp.

---

1   short form for Indian husband, often preceded by vowels like *a* and *o*

'So you also must have been like him in that age,' deduces Aunt as she makes animadversions on Uncle's adolescence and tries to exonerate her son.

'Just shut your mouth, Pushpa! Give it a rest sometimes, for God's sake!' begs hypertensed Uncle.

'I'll see both of them tomorrow. Get me a glass of water now,' Uncle tells Aunt as he goes to his room to fetch some tablets to lower his blood pressure.

Dinkar returns to his fortress of solitude unaware of the intrusion by Mayank in his absence.

He shakes the mouse and is astonished to see Chandni online. In a split second, his feelings of a sense of sexcapade transform into a burden of adultery. Few hours before, he could have given up anything to hear from Chandni once, but now his fingers quiver to type an alphabet or two as if a visit to the brothel has rendered him unworthy of Chandni. Somehow he garners courage to face Chandni.

Aaftaab123: hi

Kool_Chandni: hey! How r u buddy? Can't tell u how happy I am to see u ☺. but ur cousin is a total pig.

Aaftaab123: how do u know?? (Types alarmed Dinkar.)

Kool_Chandni: had a chat with him few hrs ago. Y don't u lock ur pc??

Aaftaab123: I juz left in a jiffy.

Kool_Chandni: hope u din go to a prostitute as he told. Like I wud believe it. lol.

Tears start rolling down Dinkar's cheeks like boulders down the hill, thence on to the keyboard. The first one drops on *S*, second on *O*, followed by *R*, again *R*, and then *Y*, as if every atom inside him were feeling guilty and repenting, only that his tears lack the momentum of boulders in order to press the keys and convey the message through to Chandni. Thereafter, the keyboard is adequately irrigated by the untimely monsoon from Dinkar's eyes. He sobs for five minutes while Chandni keeps buzzing him, anxiously fearing what Mayank told her might be true.

Kool_Chandni: R u there dinkar? Wat happened?

Kool_Chandni: ur silence isn't gonna defend u!

Kool_Chandni: ok fine..so I believe it's true. Am goin and I don wanna c u again. bye.

Dinkar gets hold of himself, seeing her fleeing. He tells her that nothing happened, and he won't do it again as he types emphatically. Wait a minute! Oh no! The keyboard isn't responding. Somebody tell Dinkar, the poor guy is just typing without looking at the screen! Probably his tears have rendered the keyboard kaput. As he realizes that his hits on the keyboard are not bearing any fruit on the screen, he begins to panic. He hits the keys repeatedly, with each hit harder than the previous one but to no avail. Then he frantically sends her all sorts of emoticons using the mouse to stop her which further pisses Chandni off.

Aaftaab123: ☺☹☺

Kool_Chandni: r u kidding me????

Kool_Chandni logged out.

And this will be the last time Dinkar sees her online. So I prophesy!

He soon realizes that there is a touch keyboard on the screen too, but it's too late as Chandni has gone offline forever and blocked him. Dinkar is distraught! The alcohol enriches his rage as he hurls the keyboard on the wall. He still isn't happy as he plays piano on it with his feet until the keys lose the will to resurge after being suppressed again and again like the poverty in this country.

Hey! Wait! What did the monitor do? And the monitor hits rock bottom too, lying adjacent to the keyboard like two lovers lying on the ground, counting their last breaths, and extending hands towards each other but unable to meet, who were half-murdered by their own for false honour as they tried to seek love outside their community. Well, in this case, it is the murderer who tried to do that!

And had it been a real mouse, it would have long escaped to its safety, but this one just waits haplessly to meet its end.

He performs the last riots as he devours the CPU and UPS too and wipes out the entire paraphernalia that was his only gateway to the outside world. And now he lies showering in his tears along with his aura of negativity, doing what he does best, lamenting, mourning, regretting, and repenting. Dinkar has lost the will to survive yet again.

He keeps staring at the obliterated hardware for a while, like a stone-sculpted idol of Ellora and then falls asleep. He is woken up in the morning by the knocking on his door. It's the auntie again, not the brothel one but his own aunt. As soon as Dinkar opens the door, she starts firing him with her verbal artillery.

'Dinkar, yesterday you crossed the limit! You misbehaved with your uncle, you . . . you . . . oh my god! What happened to your computer? Was there an earthquake last night? I did not feel any tremors! Or did you do this? Why did you do it?' blabbers the incessant aunt. Dinkar just yawns as he opens his mouth as wide as he can, returns to his bed, and pulls up the blanket to his face, turning a blind eye to the aunt. Aunt pulls his blanket with full force and holds it like a matador holding a cape in front of a raging bull. The only differences here are that there is no bull and she resembles a bulldozer.

'Get ready now. We are going to see Dr Malhotra today,' shouts Aunt.

Dinkar has lost the spunk to resist anything. He just follows his aunt's command like a robot and gets ready to be mentally dissected by his psychiatrist. They board their old Ambassador, chauffeured by their older driver, Shiv Omprakash Shukla, or SoS as they call him—rightly so because he often leaves them in a distressful situation though of a different nature. The car belonged to Dinkar's father, and they still drag it as the uncle doesn't want to spend on a new one. It hardly offers any lickety-split drive, but SoS embarrasses the car and the family even in front of the foot-powered rickshaws. He had a few mishaps in the past which has made him extra cautious and given him a tachophobia, or fear of speed. They can't fire him because they pay him peanuts. He gets really nervous when there is an open road in front of him because the aunt keeps reminding him of his score of how many bicycles have overtaken.

'Faster, SoS, for God's sake, drive a bit faster. The whole city is overtaking us. It feels as if we are going back in time!' begs the frustrated aunt.

'Wow! Did you see that!' exclaims Dinkar, as a BMW i6 shoots by like a meteor, blasting all the speed limits set by the traffic police.

'Ya, you go alive to dead in 4.6 seconds in that!' chuckles SoS. He is probably the only driver in Delhi who takes a sigh of relief on encountering a jam. He has this to say in his defence, 'Better late than late!'

They reach the clinic and thank the lord for making it on the same day. While they wait for their appointment, Aunt warns Dinkar against any insolence towards the doctor. It's really a horrifying experience to wait at a clinic with the buffet of posters around you, showcasing various diseases the human kind is capable of harbouring.

Aunt is busy in her last-minute repairs of her face while Dinkar sits there like a lamb on Bakreed. After waiting for a while, they are called in by the doctor.

'Hello, Dr Malhotra! How are you?' greets charged-up Aunt, extending her loosened up right hand with palm down as if the doctor will kiss it!

'I am fine, Mrs Chauhan! How are you? My god, you have shed a few kilos,' says the flirtatious doctor nasally, while gently squeezing her hand, though it's a wonder how someone can flirt with an ornate cow! Well, maybe a baboon-faced can!

Nevertheless, Aunt's eyes light up as her long strenuous journey finally proves fruitful. This is why she is always excited to take Dinkar to the doctor as she needs her own little doses to bolster her delusions of glamour.

'So, Dinkar, how are you doing? Long time no see. You should bring him at least once a month, Mrs Chauhan.'

'Oh! I would love to. I mean, I have no problem, but he resists a lot,' explains Aunt while concealing her excitement on the proposal.

'Why won't you see me, Dinkar? Don't you want to get better? Are you taking your medications regularly?' enquires the doctor as Dinkar goes numb, staring at his mole. He doesn't respond.

Aunt quickly jumps in. 'No, Doctor, he is not. You know what he did yesterday?' and Aunt doesn't leave the minuscule detail untold.

Doctor gets hold of himself after the heavy bombardment of information from the aunt. He prepares for the psychoanalytic therapy session of Dinkar and asks Aunt to wait outside.

Doctor asks Dinkar to lie on the couch and relax, as he pulls the shades of the window to reduce the brightness.

'So tell me, Dinkar, what's up with you lately?' asks the doctor, as Dinkar lies on the couch with a serene face and eyes shut. 'Tell me, what's going on in your mind?' Still no response from Dinkar. It seems like he has fallen asleep, as he fetched little sleep last night.

'Dinkar . . . Dinkar.' The doctor shakes him up gently. Dinkar murmurs something, turns his back towards the doctor, and goes back to sleep again as the room felt so peaceful and the couch so comfortable except for the whizzing noise that the doctor made, but that too felt like a flute today.

The doctor keeps staring at Dinkar, befuddled, and scribbles something on paper for a couple of minutes before calling for the aunt.

'That was quick, Doctor,' enquires Aunt as she grabs the chair.

'I am sorry to say this, Mrs Chauhan, but therapy won't work if Dinkar himself is not willing to get better,' tells the doctor.

'He is becoming very stubborn day by day. What should we do, Doctor? We are very worried!' sobs Aunt, shedding a few crocodile tears.

'Calm down, Mrs Chauhan,' the doctor consoles her, holding her hand across the table. Aunt closes her eyes as she receives a micro-orgasm.

'Oh, Dr Malhotra, what would I do without you? I mean, what would we do! You are our last hope for Dinkar,' shrieks Aunt, pacifying her amorous feelings.

'Well, there is only one therapy left now, considering Dinkar's condition. Many people have benefitted from it though it's a bit disputatious,' tells the doctor.

'Tell me about it, Doctor,' asks Aunt curiously.

'It's called past life regression therapy. In this we use hypnosis on the subject to recover his past life memories in order to find the root cause of his problems in the present life,' explains the doctor.

'That sounds interesting, Doctor. I can also undergo such therapy?' asks bewildered Aunt.

'Anyone can undergo such therapy, but why would you do that? You look perfectly fine to me,' says the doctor, as Aunt already starts to regress in her past life where she is a princess and Dr Malhotra her frog charming. Mercy be upon the people of the kingdom.

'If you want, I can recommend Dinkar to a fellow practitioner, who is an expert in this field.' The doctor nudges Aunt out of her musing.

'Well . . . I'll have to discuss with his uncle before making any decision,' tells Aunt.

'Let me know then when you are ready,' the doctor extends his hand for a handshake, signalling their time is up.

Aunt grabs it like a trophy with both hands. 'See you, Dr Malhotra. Always a pleasure meeting you. Bye!' she says as she keeps shaking his hand and also him.

'Mrs Chauhan, I think you are forgetting something,' reminds the doctor.

'Oh! How sweet!' She spreads her arms to hug the doctor.

'No, no, I meant Dinkar. He is still sleeping there.' The doctor rescues himself, falling back as Aunt retracts her arms embarrassingly.

'Ha ha ha, just kidding, ji.' Aunt tries to circumvent the situation.

She shakes Dinkar hard with a strident voice, and Dinkar stands up on his feet at once.

'Come, let's go, Dinkar! Did you come here to sleep? I don't know what to do with you,' freaks Aunt as Dinkar drags along. And like a professional actor, her facial muscles make a switch from an angry expression to a smiley one in a split second on catching a glimpse of Dr Malhotra.

They leave the clinic for a long journey to a place not so far away. After reaching home, Dinkar hits the sack, reminiscing Chandni, while Aunt gets busy in household chores.

Chapter 8

Game to Fame

At night after finishing with the dinner, Aunt tells Uncle about the visit to Dr Malhotra's clinic as he watches TV. 'Dr Malhotra suggested past life regeneration therapy for Dinkar. You know, ji, what is it all about?' asks Aunt proudly as she was sure she gained a certain edge in terms of knowledge over Uncle.

'It's past life regression therapy. There is a whole new show about it on television.' Uncle outsmarts Aunt.

'Which show is that?' asks excited Aunt.

'It's called *Raaz Pichhle Janam Ka* [*The Secret of Past Life*]. It airs on weekdays at 9 p.m.,' informs Uncle.

'Play, play . . . play that channel. It's 9.15 now.' Aunt snatches the remote from Uncle emphatically and searches for the popular channel sacrificing her daily soap.

The show is on. A man lies half-asleep on a white bed amidst a surreal ambience. A doctor, who is conducting the therapy, asks him questions about his past life, which he answers as if murmuring while sleeping. A movie is shown too side by side on the basis of his information. His family watches him from a distance, seated on a couch with the show host, who is a popular Bollywood star.

The thought of being on the show with Dinkar charges the aunt. She starts imagining herself on that couch in the studio, alongside this superstar and the show host.

'Let's go on this show, ji. We will be famous. My friends will be so jealous,' says uplifted Aunt.

'Ya, right! Like they are waiting for us,' taunts Uncle. 'Besides, all this is drama. It's just fake.'

'No, no, believe me, it works. Dr Malhotra told me, it's our last resort. Let's try at least. If they won't call us, well and good. What's the harm in trying? I have a very strong feeling that we are going to become famous!' Aunt tries to persuade Uncle.

'Don't eat my brains, Pushpa. We have always suffered whenever you had a strong feeling in the past! No means no. If Dinkar has to undergo therapy, let it be done at a clinic, not on some lame show,' declares Uncle, blocking her road to glory and fame.

At night, the aunt keeps rolling to and fro, side to side on her part of the bed, as Uncle snores away adjacently. She is unable to sleep, dreaming about being on the show, planning what suit and jewellery to wear, shaking the hand of the Bollywood star, and boasting later in front of the jealous neighbours and friends, as she was going to call the producers anyway in spite of her husband's reluctance.

Next day, as soon as Uncle leaves for his work, she begins the covert operation of booking a seat for Dinkar on the show.

She collects information from the Internet about the show. She makes a few calls and enquires about the procedure to participate in the show. They advise her to fill a form online and attach the medical history of Dinkar. She asks for Mayank's assistance and mails the documents as required. Her job done, now all she has to do is wait for their call and think of ways to persuade Uncle, which wasn't going to be difficult after all these years of experience. If needed, she could use her Brahmastra, the golden arrow given by the almighty to all womankind against which the mightiest of men feel helpless—i.e. the tears. That is the reason why late Rajesh Khanna used to say, 'Pushpa . . . I hate tears!'

Dinkar turns eco-friendly and decides not to waste paper and starts scribbling on the walls of his room instead.

Abhi main jawaan hi to hoon,

Ek dil ka zakhm-o-nishaan hi to hoon.

I am still young only,

Just a wound and a scar of a heart.

Chamaktaa hoon bheegi aankhon me magar,

Ek adhooraa saa armaan hi to hoon.

I glisten in the moist eyes but

I am just an unfulfilled yearning.

Kyun jud rahe hain har pal log naye,

Main ghamon ka kaarvaan hi to hoon.

Why are people joining me every moment,

I am just a caravan of grief.

Bikhar jaaunga ek din toot kar tumhi pe,

Tumhaare khwaabon ka aasmaan hi to hoon.

I will break and shatter one day on you only,

I am the sky of your dreams.

Mujh se bach kar jaaoge kahan,

Main saara jahan hi to hoon.

Where would you escape from me,

I am the whole world itself.

Bahot huaa ke ab mita do mujhe,

Do dilon ke darmiyaan hi to hoon.

Erase me as it has been enough,

I am between the two hearts only.

Another impediment between Aunt and her dream is Dinkar himself. Aunt knows how stubborn Dinkar is, but she is equally determined and vows to haul Dinkar along if required.

She softly knocks on Dinkar's door. When she doesn't get any response after knocking repeatedly and lovingly calling out Dinkar's name, she pushes the door open. She is dumbfounded at the sight of his room and all the graffiti Dinkar made. He is busy acting deaf while decorating the floor, as all other accessible areas were already full.

'Dinkar, beta [son], that was such an expensive paint. All walls are ruined now,' exclaims Aunt softly, while suppressing her anger and faking affection. 'You enjoy annoying your aunt, don't you?'

Dinkar continues scribbling on the floor, not at all interested in what his aunt has to say, as she tries to explain to him the little she knows about the therapy and more about the show and the name and the fame.

'This time I don't want to hear any excuses. You have to come when they call us, okay?' tells Aunt, awaiting Dinkar's agreement.

Apparently, Dinkar is in a parallel universe where sound from this world is not able to penetrate.

'Okay, Dinkar?' she asks again and a bit louder this time, trying to cross over to his plane.

'Ya, ya, whatever!' says Dinkar, irritated as Aunt manages to find a wormhole.

A big smile pops up on her face, with fireworks in her eyes, as she crosses one more hurdle. She wants to take it in writing, on stamped paper, from Dinkar lest he refuses afterwards, but for now she takes his word no matter how tentative it sounded.

A week passes by as Aunt anxiously waits to hear from the channel and show organizers. Today is her lucky day. It's 15 August 2018, the Independence Day. The whole of Delhi is closed, and Uncle is at home too, enjoying the prime minister's address to the nation on TV, seated on his black leather sofa in his living room with his legs stretched and firmly placed on the centre table. Adjacent to his feet lies a vase full of fresh flowers counting their last few breaths due to his stinking socks.

A phone kept on the corner table adjacent to the sofa interrupts the proceedings. Uncle cries out for Aunt to pick up the phone as he is too busy watching TV, whereas the aunt is in the kitchen, preparing breakfast for him. Aunt hurries out of the kitchen to answer the phone with her one hand soaked in wheat flour.

'You cannot even move a hand,' cribs Aunt as she comes out of the kitchen, clearing the hair falling on her face and tucking them behind her ear while unwittingly smearing her whole face with the wheat flour.

She clears her throat as she picks up the receiver and melodifies her husky voice, 'Hello!'

For next few minutes, all one could hear is 'Ya . . . Thank you! . . . Ya . . . Thank you!' After each thank you, the grin on her face keeps expanding until it meets her ears. Finally, she disconnects the call with an extra large 'Thank you so much!' Maybe she would have added a 'mmuaahhh' after that if Uncle wasn't there.

After the call gets disconnected, Aunt holds the receiver close to her heart and falls on the sofa, feeling too weak in her knees to stand, but in doing so, she lands her bum on Uncle's thighs, who is just sitting adjacently, waiting for his favourite part of the parade, the gun salute.

And boom, all guns go blazing in the background.

As he agonizingly cries her name, 'Pushpaaa', she jumps back on her feet again, realizing the ground was not clear.

'Oooh . . . what the hell is wrong with you?' shouts Uncle, frantically massaging his thighs.

'Aaah,' cries Uncle again, petrified as she turns to him with her flour-smeared face resembling a witch.

'We got selected for the show!' Aunt giggles while joining hands to thank God as she sprinkles salt on Uncle's wound.

'Selected? What? Where?' enquires perplexed Uncle.

The past life regression therapy one. Arre that *Raaz Pichhle Janam Ka*, that show, they invited us, balle balle!' Aunt celebrates while doing bhangra, the Punjabi folk dance. 'We are going to get famous, yippee!'

'I told you to forget about that show! You don't listen.'

As Uncle begins to scold her, she cuts him short and interrupts in between. 'Do you have any idea how expensive this therapy is? Firstly, they will do it for free. Secondly [most importantly], we will be on national television! How many people get that kind of chance!' argues the insistent aunt.

The monetary thing clicks with Uncle as he gives his tacit approval. 'Do whatever you want to do, but you will be responsible if anything goes wrong. And wash your face!'

'Oho . . . you don't worry, ji. I will manage everything,' consoles the motivated and exuberant aunt while wiping her face with her dupatta (a long scarf).

Now she has to just sit back in a beauty parlour and wait for the final call. She undergoes an intensive beauty treatment regime and follows a rigorous diet plan to look her best. She enrols herself in a nearby gymnasium to lose some fat. She receives the final call after a fortnight. The day is fixed. The day that will change their lives forever, especially that of Dinkar! She prepares a list of each and every relative, friend, and neighbour, as if for her son's wedding invitation, and calls them up one by one to broadcast about her appearance on the show.

Chapter 9

The Anti-Clock

Finally, the big day arrives. It's 3 September, and a chauffeured car sent by the show organizers waits in front of the house.

Except Dinkar, everyone else seems superexcited, and they dress like they never dressed before. Uncle and Mayank look dapper in their newly stitched grey-and-black coat pants, and Aunt is all glittery and dazzling in her heavily gemmed green salwar suit and matching jewellery. Dinkar just manages to find a decent blue striped shirt and black trousers.

They board the car as they embark upon the life-changing journey. Uncle sits in front with the driver while the other three at the rear with Aunt providing segregation between the two incompatible and dangerous goods.

Dinkar lowers the windowpane as he feels cold due to the car air con running. Mayank immediately objects. 'Close the window, you moron. AC is running.'

Uncle seconds that and asks Dinkar to close the window as they all are sweating in their blazers. Aunt mediates lest

Dinkar jumps out of the car. They finally agree to lower the air con a tad bit, and Dinkar raises the glass. Aunt blabbers on for the rest of the journey, lecturing the family about how not to let fame get to their heads.

An hour later, they arrive at the studio in Noida Film City. Everyone is bedazzled alike to see the huge set and the lights and the area beyond the sets not seen on TV. There is an elevated stage in the centre, round in shape, lit from beneath in white light, and in the middle lies a retractable couch for the participant. There is a large, about six feet tall, imposing analogue clock on the wall adjacent to the stage, ticking anticlockwise. In front of the stage lies another podium on the right with a sofa and a centre table for the family members and the host to be seated, and then finally, there is this arena for the studio audience.

The Chauhans are briefed by the crew about the dos and don'ts, while Aunt is asked to shed some jewellery and a few bangles off her arms as this was not Dinkar's swayamvar (one of the shows where you participate to seek a bride). Aunt reluctantly abides, cursing the director as she paid a hefty amount to get dressed from a beauty parlour and rented out the jewellery.

Soon after, the family is greeted by the lady doctor who is to conduct the therapy. She has few words with Dinkar, and surprisingly, Dinkar behaves well and seems excited too. Though she gets a little uncomfortable with the aunt who keeps on touching her to make sure she wasn't dreaming. Uncle and Aunt seem very pleased seeing Dinkar cooperating. By this time, Mayank has already been warned twice or thrice by the crew against posing in front of cameras and interrupting with the proceedings.

Then arrives the host. The aunt goes berserk over his one glimpse. The director comes to his rescue, and the family is instructed to be seated on the sofa. After all the studio audience is seated, the director gives a go ahead.

It's time to roll the cameras for the opening shot. Loud music plays, and all sorts of colourful lights flicker as the host appears amidst the fog on the stage in front of the large clock. He opens the show with the following lines, 'Namaskar, Aadaab, Satsriakaal. Here we are on yet another journey back in time. I am ready, you are ready, whole Hindustan is ready. It's time to turn the clocks in the opposite direction. Today we have with us Dinkar Chauhan who has had a very troubled childhood and adolescence and is here to seek some answers by regressing to his past life. His uncle, auntie, and cousin are here to support him. Let's know more about Dinkar from them.'

One camera points at the Chauhans, and 'Cut', shouts the director. There is an unusually large grin on Aunt's face, and she waved towards the camera as she was being introduced. The director advises her to try to look more serious and concerned.

They roll back again as the host enquires about Dinkar from Uncle. Aunt jumps in without invitation and begins her storytelling from scratch (when Uncle came to see her for marriage) like a priest reciting hymns from Mahabharat. The director interjects again as her documentary alone would run through the entire length of the show. After a few retakes, they wrap up the introductory part with lot of work to do at the editing table.

Now the main show, Dinkar's past life regression begins. He is asked to lie down on the bed at the centre of the stage. Everyone is advised to maintain pin-drop silence until the next forty to fifty minutes as the doctor hypnotizes Dinkar and helps him to go into a semi-conscious state. Everyone waits anxiously as forty-five minutes pass by, and the doctor signals to the cameras that it's about time to begin the show. She gently taps on Dinkar's cheeks as she asks, 'Dinkar, can you hear me?'

'Hmmm', mumbles Dinkar while eyes closed but eyelids fluttering.

'Just relax and go back to your childhood. Go back. Go back. Go back,' guides the doctor as her voice gradually fades away in the lull. 'Now you are in your childhood. Tell me, where are you?'

'Mhtrhk', speaks Dinkar incoherently. The doctor gently nudges him again. 'Yes, go on, Dinkar! Where are you?'

'It's a market. Very crowded,' speaks Dinkar a bit clearly this time while eyes wide shut.

'Who are you with, Dinkar?' asks the doctor.

'Mom and Dad,' informs Dinkar with a blooming face and a vibrant voice. I am sure his eyes must be glittering too under those eyelids.

'What are you doing?' enquires the doctor again.

'Shopping . . . eating . . . balloons . . . and . . . and . . .' Suddenly the expressions take a turn on his face. He looks terrified and shaky and now in horror. The doctor tries to comfort him. 'Calm down, Dinkar, calm down, tell me, what happened?' asks the doctor as spectators are on the edge of their seats, except Mayank, who is all laid-back and smirking. What an idiot.

'Explosion . . . every . . . everything is finished,' tells Dinkar as tears surface on the periphery of his eyes.

'Relax, Dinkar. I want you to go back, beyond this life, in a previous life, find a happy memory, go back . . . go back . . . go back,' tells the doctor.

Dinkar's expressions again shift gears, and now he has that serene look.

'Tell me, Dinkar, what do you see?' asks the doctor.

'Mountains', tells a sparky Dinkar.

'Do you know what place it is?' enquires the doctor.

'Kashmir . . . Azad Kashmir', proclaims Dinkar slowly.

In India, it's known as PoK or Pakistan-occupied Kashmir. The director's eyes light up as he knows already the TRP is going to soar. And this is the longest Auntie has ever gone without speaking in brief history of time.

'Who are you? What's your name?' asks the doctor.

'Aaftaab,' replies Dinkar in a feeble tone.

That's the pseudonym Dinkar has always used in his ghazals and while chatting. Now it's time for Mayank to be on the edge of his seat as he is familiar with this name.

'Okay, Aaftaab, tell me, what do you do?' asks the doctor.

'Training', replies Dinkar.

'What training is it for?' enquires the doctor again.

'Mission . . . in India . . . New Delhi', mumbles Dinkar.

'What mission is it? Tell me, Aaftaab,' nudges the doctor as Dinkar seems to fall asleep.

'Parliament . . . attack Indian parliament,' informs Dinkar.

The whole studio goes numb for a minute as if they have seen a ghost. Uncle and Aunt look towards each other in consternation and so does everyone else, including the doctor. It was like cracking the seventeen-year-old case. Mayank learns he is badly screwed, as he locked horns with a bull instead of a deer, and begins to perspire.

The doctor looks at the director with seeking eyes, asking whether to continue or not. The director nods his head in approval, and why not!

The doctor continues to interrogate Dinkar as she gently taps on his face again. 'When is it going to happen, Dinkar? The attack on Indian parliament?'

She realizes she addressed him wrong and quickly reiterates. 'Aaftaab! Can you hear me? When are you planning to attack the parliament?' asks the doctor as she taps Dinkar's cheeks softly.

'Terah . . . terah disambar [13 December],' murmurs Dinkar.

'Why are you doing this?' asks the doctor.

'Jan . . . Jannat naseeb hogi . . . bahattar hooren milengi [I will get entry in paradise, will receive seventy-two virgins].'

Uncle gives a rebuking look to Aunt, as if saying, 'See, I told you not to do this, but you never listen to me.'

The doctor proceeds further. 'Now go to the day of attack. Three . . . two . . . and when I will say one, it will be 13 December. And one. It's 13 December today. Tell me, Aaftaab, what do you see? Tell me, where are you now, Aaftaab? Come on, tell me, where are you?' asks the doctor in a commanding tone as she helps Dinkar fast-forward to the D-day. The perplexed audience watches it without blinking, including Mayank.

'We are entering the parliament through a gate,' stutters Dinkar with a wrinkled face as he breathes heavily.

'How many people are there with you?' asks the doctor.

'Four,' replies Dinkar.

'Which car are you driving?' asks the doctor.

Dinkar turns his head to the right and replies jadedly, 'White . . . Ambassador', as if he could see everything happening around him.

'What weapons are you carrying?' asks the doctor.

'AK-47 . . . grenades . . . pistols . . . and . . . and . . .' informs Dinkar as he gasps for breath and turns his head side to side.

'And? Tell me, Aaftaab, what else?' asks the doctor while wiping sweat off his forehead.

'And . . . I am wearing a suicide vest!' tells Dinkar.

And everyone who is on the edge of their seats lean back, as if Dinkar really is wearing one. Aunt digs her nails deep in the cushion of her seat in fear of the repercussions following the broadcast of the episode.

'Tell me what happens once you are inside!' asks the doctor.

'We are intercepted by the police. We get off the car and start firing. Gunshots everywhere. We run to take cover,' shouts Dinkar as his throat dries up and droplets resurface on his face.

Doctor instructs again with a firm voice, 'Go further, Aaftaab, what do you see now? Tell me.'

'I . . . I . . . I am shot. My . . . my vest explodes . . . I am dead!' says frightened Dinkar while shaking and frantically swaying his head at first and then suddenly pacifying as if really dead.

Everyone in the studio appears horrified as they watch with their mouths open. Mayank seems scared as he thinks the first thing Dinkar will do after waking up is beat his ass.

The doctor conducts the closing ceremony. 'Now slowly your consciousness will rise out of your body. What do you see?'

'There is no body. Only mutilated body parts. It looks terrible!' shrieks Dinkar as tears roll down his eyes towards his ears. And as emotions spread like a communicable disease, Aunt and Uncle catch it too and shed a few tears.

'How do you feel?' asks the doctor, quite similar to a news reporter asking a victim of communal violence who is lying on a hospital bed and his broken leg suspended in mid air. 'So how do you feel after this attack?' 'Oh, I feel wonderful. It's great fun lying here the whole day. You should try it too sometimes.' That's what I would have replied to these reporters if I were in their place. But in this case, the doctor's question does make sense.

'Dejected. Dispirited. Unwanted,' replies Dinkar remorsefully.

'Do you see paradise?' asks the doctor.

'No . . . nowhere near . . . only vast emptiness everywhere. Inside and outside,' replies Dinkar.

'Okay. Now you will leave all the sadness, dejection, and remorse there with that body. Feel it as it's destroyed with that body. Your consciousness will now enter this body through the skin without any sadness and regret. I will count from three to one, and on one, you will slowly open your eyes. Three, two, and one,' directs the therapist.

Dinkar slowly opens his eyes and regains full consciousness. 'Cut', shouts the director, and it's time for a break beyond which the show will be wrapped up post an interview with Dinkar.

Dinkar feels as if rising after a hibernation of years and has shed a great load from his head as it appears light. Uncle and Aunt appear to have sniffed chloroform, while Mayank shakes his legs interminably.

After having a glass of water, Dinkar gets ready with rest of the family to be interviewed by the host about his experience. He is seated on the sofa with the other three as the host on the adjacent seat interviews Dinkar.

'How do you feel after this journey back in time? Did you get answers you were seeking?' asks the host.

'I feel exhausted, but it really was a great experience. I feel a strange but pleasant calmness inside me. I think now I know answers to many questions that I sought all life long. I must thank my auntie for bringing me here,' chatters on Dinkar, probably the first time in his life. And Auntie does not know whether to feel proud or curse herself for bringing him here as she can hear Uncle's blood bubbling up.

'What do you think about this whole experience? How helpful was it?' The host turns on to the family.

For the first time, Aunt's tongue was struggling to form syllables, let alone the words.

'Goo . . . good experience, sir. Shocking but helpful. We never treated Dinkar any different than our own son. He he he!' Aunt grins nervously.

'I don't have words. It was very moving for me,' exclaims Uncle emotionally. So moving that he may have to move out of Delhi soon.

'Well, that was the journey of Dinkar Chauhan to his past life and back. Join us next week as we take someone else on this amazing journey back in time. Good night, shubh ratri, shabba khair,' concludes the host as everyone erupts in applause. 'Cut', calls the director, and the crew begins to wrap up.

The show is over, but for the Chauhans, it is just the curtain raiser. After expressing regards and bidding adieus to the team of the show, the Chauhans board their ride home.

Though it's past midnight, none of them feel dizzy except the driver. No one dares to utter a word though each one has at least a thousand questions sprouting in their heads. Dinkar feels the chill again and asks to stop the air con. Surprisingly, everyone endeavours to please him as Uncle stops the air con and the other two lower their windowpanes in a jiffy lest he blows himself up again, or who knows, he still may have contacts. Dinkar is the new uncrowned king now.

Chapter 10

The Quiet before the Storm

After they reach home, they all retire to their respective rooms. Uncle starts snoring as soon as he falls on the bed while Aunt gets busy winding up the jewellery exhibition she has been displaying all day and later scrapes off the make-up from her face. As she sits there in front of the mirror and her concealed face begins to resurface, she gets the wind of reality. What will happen once the show gets aired? What will people say? How will she answer them? Her dream of making her friends and neighbours jealous gets washed up with her make-up. She could not sleep thereafter. Mayank bolts, latches, and locks his door as there is a terrorist in the house.

Dinkar, on the other hand, is bewildered at the journey he just came back from, in time! 'Is it for real?' he asks himself again and again. Was he really Aaftaab in his previous life? Was he really capable of killing someone other than himself, although he did think about murdering Mayank once or twice, but then who hasn't? We all want to kill someone or the other at different stages of our lives in the heat of the moment when they annoy us to the core. To think of killing someone is just human; to act on it is a job of a beast.

Was it just a coincidence that he used Aaftaab as a pseudonym in his ghazals? Maybe it was all just a sham, plotted by his subconscious mind. Nevertheless, he chooses to believe that it is true as it is the most convenient thing to do under the circumstances and also relieves him of his karmic debt. Now he knows exactly how he got screwed. Amidst this swirling in a whirlpool of thoughts, Dinkar manages to catch some sleep but not for long.

He is woken again by that recurring nightmare. A masked man wearing a turban appears again. He carries a Kalashnikov in one hand and holds a red-coloured button in the other hand, which is connected to the suicide vest he is wearing through a network of wires. But today it came with additional twenty seconds of never-before-seen footage. Before blowing himself up, he removes the cloth covering his face and reveals himself. Dinkar is shocked to the core as he sees his face. He could not believe that the person whom he dreaded the most, the one who made him shiver and sweat all at the same time, in the middle of night, all through his life, was none other than himself. Yes, it was his own face beneath the veil, slightly bearded, with piercing eyes. He slowly places his thumb on the red button. Suddenly Dinkar's consciousness transcends into the terrorist's body whereas earlier Dinkar used to watch him from a distance. As he goes for pressing the red button, Dinkar flounders in his sleep, trying to stop himself from pressing the button but doesn't succeed. He wakes up panting. He feels a burning sensation in his whole body, and his throat feels so dry as if he were dying of thirst, like a traveller who spent several days wandering in a desert in scorching heat.

The therapy does help Dinkar as he begins to value life. He regularly strolls out in the evening and spends hours sitting on a bench in a nearby park. It's very crowded and bustles with activity. He observes people of all ages, children playing on swings and slides, young ones jogging, older ones walking, and the really old sitting in a corner and singing bhajans (devotional songs). Strangely, now Dinkar feels more peaceful here compared to the solitude of his room.

The day the episode is going to telecast quietly arrives without much happening in between. It is the quiet before the storm. The anxiety usually starts from the stomach in the form of butterflies or acid reflux and then spreads to hands, feet, and finally shows on the face. Uncle and Aunt experience the same while Dinkar is unaware that it was today! If everything would have gone well, Aunt would have been broadcasting all around the neighbourhood with a loud hailer about the show, but now she just prays that at least near and dear ones somehow give it a miss. If there were a tantric ritual for hailing the magnetic storm in order to interrupt the satellite signals, she would have performed it while standing on one leg. That's how much she wants this thing to go off air. But what's going to happen will happen!

The same evening, Aunt apprises Uncle of her feeling of uneasiness. 'I am not feeling good, ji. Let's go somewhere out of Delhi for a few days.'

'Ohho . . . you only wanted to go on that show, and I warned you then. Now you want to run away from all this? Just sit back and enjoy the name and fame you wanted,' tells the infuriated uncle with a pinch of sarcasm.

We all hate when that happens! Someone tells you not to do something out of habit, but you still go ahead and do it. Then unfortunately, it doesn't work out without any fault of yours. That's when these people seize the chance without fail and make you realize again and again that you committed a blunder because you did not heed their advice. As if they knew you were going to get screwed.

Aunt doesn't dare to say one more word and gulps the bitter truth.

It's 5 October 2018, 9 p.m. Aunt, Uncle, and Mayank gather in the living room after dinner to witness their first ever television appearance. Dinkar isn't interested and limits himself to the walls of his room.

As soon as the show starts, the whole family appears on the screen. Their faces light up, seeing themselves on national television, and everybody smiles as they look towards one another. Soon the aunt starts whining about her footage getting cropped as Uncle shushes her up.

As the show progresses, Aunt's heartbeat rises. She keeps looking at the phone, fearing people might start calling any minute now. Dinkar's story is enacted and shown in the form of a movie simultaneously as he reveals it under hypnosis. The episode concludes at 10 p.m., and by now, even Uncle starts feeling fidgety. He asks Aunt for an antacid after which he heads to his bedroom. Uncle gradually falls asleep while sceptically pondering about tomorrow. Soon the room reverberates with his snores. Aunt keeps checking the phone, frequently peeping from the corner of her eye over her shoulder as it is kept perpendicularly across on the table. She thinks it will really start ringing if she looks at it directly. Later than sooner, she falls asleep too.

But not for long as they are disturbed by the ringing of the phone, which the aunt had been ghastly expecting. Aunt quickly lights the table lamp. The phone keeps ringing as Uncle and Aunt look towards each other in a quagmire, whether to pick it up and answer or keep it off the hook. Uncle steps up to answer as there was no silent button on this one. He clears his throat and throws a hello into the receiver.

A guy replies with a question. 'Hello, is this Dinkar Chauhan's residence?'

'Who are you?' asks Uncle.

'I am calling from ANI news agency,' replies the guy.

Uncle hangs off and the receiver goes off the hook. Soon their mobile phones start ringing too. Uncle hurriedly switches them off too.

'Bloody news channels have started calling,' yells the agitated uncle. 'I knew it. See, this is what happens when you don't listen to your husband. Congrats! We are famous now!' tells Uncle sarcastically, as Aunt tries to hide her face under the blanket and acts sleepy. Uncle switches off the lamp, and they struggle to sleep thereafter.

Chapter 11

Oh No! We are famous

In the morning, Uncle and Aunt are woken up by the doorbell. It rings a few times until Uncle realizes that it isn't a dream and its ringing is for real. He extends his arm to the side and nudges Aunt to go and answer the door. Aunt lifts herself out of the bed with quite a lot of effort and looks at the clock tick-tocking on the opposite wall as she squints her eyes and tries to focus. She curses the person ringing the bell at this hour, as it is 6.15 a.m. while they are used to getting up around 6.30 a.m. She limps to the door as her legs have not woken up fully. As she opens the door and peeps out, she is greeted by an unexpected crowd of reporters and cameramen, who stand at a distance of a few yards from her, just behind the iron gate. She freezes for a minute in a daze, like an ice-sculpted hippo.

All of them at once start competing to put their mikes through the grills of the gate towards the aunt, as if selling them, 'Take mine, take mine' or 'Buy this one'. Their cameramen also fight amongst themselves for a spot to take a clear shot of the aunt, yet others with still cameras start flashing unceasingly.

They all pounce at her and hurl a thousand questions.

'Is there any truth in Dinkar's story?'

'Ma'am, did you know already what Dinkar revealed on the show?'

'Is he still in contact with them?'

'Was this all a set-up to garner TRP for the show?'

'Where is Dinkar? Can we talk to him?'

Gosh! These guys! Didn't they learn in school that you should ask questions one by one?

Aunt could hardly open her eyes amid all flashing, and she quickly retreats back into the house and locks the door. She feels too weak to stand and, with her back resting on the door, slowly slides down on to the floor with her hands on her head. Uncle comes out of the room, rubbing his eyes, with his underpants' drawstring hanging between the legs, and asks who it was. He skips a beat as he sees his wife meditating on the floor by the door in a yoga asana yet to be named.

'What happened? Who is it? What are you doing sitting there?' Uncle hurls more questions at her in a matter of a few seconds than collectively asked by all the reporters outside. He quickly pulls off the curtain of the front-facing window and, with the same speed, pulls it back on again. He is equally stunned to see the crowd of reporters and cameramen lurching on the main gate like cockroaches—but not as much as Aunt to sit on the floor, so he rests on the couch instead. Hearing the commotion, Mayank too emerges out of his room and is baffled to see his parents lying here and there holding their heads.

'What happened?' he asks his father. Mr Chauhan doesn't reply and just points towards the window. Mayank too goes and peeps out of the window through the space between the curtains.

'Whoa!' exclaims Mayank with a wicked grin. 'So many of them. We are famous!'

The grin soon vaporizes as it meets his father's fiery red eyes. This exchange of unpleasantries is interrupted by a caterwaul, that of the aunt. She starts crying while beating her head and chest with her bare hands, an old classic style of weeping developed by Indian women to intimidate any and every suspecting soul. Mayank and his father soon rush towards the aunt and console her, lest the reporters misconstrue it as an act of terrorism by Dinkar. They somehow help her get on her feet and make her comfortable on the sofa. Mayank gives her water to drink as she continues sobbing while Uncle just scans the wall for a smooth spot where he can bang his head repeatedly. It is a cunning master stroke played by the aunt to take the heat off her. Now the uncle will ruminate a hundred times before blaming the aunt.

'I knew from the beginning there was something sinister about Dinkar,' blurts Mayank.

And everyone nods in. 'Hmmmmm.'

It is better to blame Dinkar than fight among one another.

Meanwhile, Dinkar wakes up too and comes out on his balcony. He is also amazed to see so many reporters at his gate and about ten satellite vans parked in line on the opposite side of the road in front of their house. As soon as they see Dinkar, everybody goes crazy, as if he were a superstar and they were his fans waiting outside for hours for his one glimpse. The cameras start flashing while reporters launch their questions from the ground towards Dinkar on the first floor. Dinkar too decides that it is better to stay indoors and goes back and lies down again on his bed.

To add to the family's misery, their maid fails to turn up today as the family did not have any resident maid after Nandini. Probably, she came but could not find a way in. Uncle too suffers as he doesn't get his newspaper, though the top headlines will be concerning Dinkar only. He forgets about going to office while Aunt forgets to prepare breakfast as everyone loses the appetite or else is too scared to ask her. Dinkar has never been too interested in eating meals. If you give him, he will eat; else he will never ask or complain.

After spending half an hour in remorse, Uncle switches on the television. Every news channel is covering Dinkar's story. Its breaking news flashing right at the bottom of the screen: Delhi boy claims to be one of the attackers of parliament in past life on a reality show. In the background, the clips from the show are being played. Uncle switches to the next channel, then the next, and the next, and so on, and every channel is covering the same news. Some of the channels even show the reporters covering the news live from outside their house. The moment when Dinkar is caught on camera on the balcony is played again and again by several channels. When news channels play a clip repeatedly for hours, it's like they are insulting our intellect, as if they think we are so slow that we do not grasp it in the first attempt.

'What is this idiot doing on the balcony?' cries Uncle.

Some channels have even started polls, asking people, 'Should Dinkar Chauhan be arrested and interrogated? For yes, type A, and for no, type B, and send it to 52525.'

Soon '#Iattackedparliament' and '#Raazpichhlejanamka' become the top trends on Facebook and Twitter. Thank God Dinkar doesn't have a Facebook account, or else it would have been flooded by the hate messages from all over India. Maybe one or two fake accounts would have emerged by now. There are people who do that just for the heck of it.

The matter would have echoed in parliament too, but it is not in session. Nevertheless, it was served on a silver platter to masala-frenzy Indian media. By afternoon, the news channels start holding debates on the issue, bifurcating television screens in six to eight windows. The guests, not as distinguished as you would think, varies from a psychiatrist, a politician from an opposition party, a Hindu religious preacher or dharm-guru alias swamiji, a maulana, and an expert sceptic.

The anchor of the show asks swamiji first about his opinion on the matter.

The guru, clad in saffron cloth and wearing rudraksh beads necklace, explains to him that as per Shrimad Bhagavad-Gita and the theory of karma, we are all born and reborn again and again and endure pain or reap happiness as per our deeds in the previous life. It is a possibility that what

Dinkar has told on the show may be true though he cannot attest the credibility of the past life regression therapy. If there is any truth in it, Dinkar should be punished for his heinous act of terrorism.

The anchor turns to the maulana and asks for his opinion. The maulana, in a white turban with a quintessential beard, argues that Islam and its followers do not believe in the theory of reincarnation and instead believe in Qayaamat, or the Day of Judgement, when the dead will resurrect and will be punished and rewarded by Allah according to their deeds. The maulana further adds that it's all a big sham and an attempt to malign Islam and its followers by Dinkar and the makers of the show, and all of them should be punished for blasphemy.

There is a rare conformity in the opinions of two learned scholars of religion as they both want Dinkar to be punished but for different reasons. If God will punish us for our deeds, then why are we punished here? Why these courts and prison? Why do they want an unfortunate teenage boy to be penalized further?

Now it is the turn of the politician from the opposition party. He begins with criticizing the ruling party regarding the worsening security situation and heightened risk of threat from terrorism in the country. The anchor interrupts and reminds him of the real agenda and asks him to restrict his opinion to the same due to limited time. The politician says that he was coming to the same point. The government should act promptly on this matter and arrest Dinkar and interrogate him so that truth shall come out. It is a matter of national security. The anchor interrupts again as it is time for a commercial break.

Post break segment, the anchor turns to the psychiatrist, who himself has conducted many such therapies, for his view. The psychiatrist throws light on the PLR (past life regression) and says that he watched the show and he believes that whatever the subject told, he has told it in a state of hypnosis and could not fabricate a story and hence must be telling the truth. He concludes that there is no doubt in his mind that Dinkar was Aaftaab in his previous life.

The expert sceptic, who was quietly listening until now, breaks his silence and interjects that there is no truth in such therapies and people are fooled in their name. Scientifically, it cannot be proven and neither can the results be duplicated, even in a controlled environment. The psychiatrist argues that not everything can be explained in terms of science and that some things are still beyond its realm.

The sceptic chuckles and says he can bet anything on it that Dinkar will not tell the same story if he underwent the therapy again. He has investigated many cases of PLR before, and all turned out to be fantasies.

The argument gets heated up, and the anchor finds it hard to maintain order.

The psychiatrist asks the sceptic, if it wasn't true, then how come Dinkar was born on 13 December 2001, the day that Aaftaab died and parliament was attacked? He also added that one terrorist indeed died in the same way as Dinkar narrated under hypnosis.

To this the sceptic replies that it's just a coincidence, nothing else. Dinkar probably read about it on the Internet as he must have known that his date of birth coincides with the parliament attack. No reports have been confirmed until now if there were any terrorists named Aaftaab involved in the attack. Also Dinkar's parents died in a terrorist attack, so these things played on his mind since childhood, and his mind came up with a story under hypnosis.

The doctor attacks him by saying that what people cannot explain, they attribute to chance and coincidence. It's an argument of convenience. At this juncture, the guru also jumps in and tells the psychiatrist that he has erred in his logic because the subtle body or soul enters the womb in between third to seventh month of pregnancy and not on the day of birth; hence, if Aaftaab died the same day, it cannot be Dinkar.

The sceptic, out of habit, opposes again and says that this is a baseless argument by the Hindu preacher, and they cannot prove that either, though the guru acted in his defence.

The swami gets agitated and warns him not to question the beliefs of the sanatana dharma, or eternal order on earth, and upset the feelings of its followers.

The politician quickly reacts and says that it's the result of unsecular and right-wing policies of the government that basic fundamental rights of expression and speech of minority are being encroached upon.

Amid all this chaos, the anchor announces the end of the debate as one could hardly hear any of them because all spoke at the same time. Debate is a method of formally presenting an argument in a disciplined manner, but not here. Irrespective of the issue, each participant comes with his own premeditated thought and agenda, howsoever irrelevant, and spouts it out unashamedly on national television. Instead of throwing light on the real issue, it's left light years behind.

The Chauhans have become prisoners in their own house. They don't allow anyone in, and neither can they step out. Aunt decides to prepare lunch as it is afternoon, and she could not bear the hungry looks on her husband's and son's faces any more. She prepares easy-to-make khichdi made from rice and lentils. Uncle keeps peeping through the curtains to keep a check on the situation outside. The reporters and camera crew are exhausted by now and cease to linger at their gate and wait in their vans across the road. Uncle takes a sigh of relief as he thinks media has left.

He asks Mayank to go to the gate and check whether anyone is there. Mayank refuses right away, saying he has not showered yet and is not ready to pose in front of the cameras as if he were a Bollywood actress without make-up.

Uncle pulls whatever little hair left on his scalp and curses his wife for that unfruitful son she bore. He ties his robe zealously like a wrestler getting ready to enter the arena. Uncle slowly and stealthily reaches the gate and peers through in all directions. Suddenly the reporters appear in front of him out of nowhere. This scares him as he retreats back, like water from the shore after a high wave. In doing so, he loses balance and falls on the ground on his hips and cameras capture the perfect shot. Uncle hurriedly gets up with one hand on his hip and hobbles back inside the house.

'Haaye, Pushpa,' he cries as he enters inside with one hand still on his hip, resembling a coward who fled from the battlefield without putting up a fight.

Aunt could not hear his husband's wail between the whistling of the pressure cooker.

'What happened, Papa?' asks Mayank.

'Fell down,' cries Uncle while resting his bruised butt on the sofa's cushion.

'Ha ha ha,' laughs Mayank.

'Shut up, idiot!' shouts Uncle.

Mayank puts a finger on his lips and continues laughing inside.

Aunt comes out of the kitchen and asks irritatingly, 'Now what happened, ji? Why are you shouting?'

'I fell down on our porch, and this idiot is laughing,' complains Uncle.

'When, why, how?' asks the bewildered aunt.

'This is how,' tells Mayank, pointing her to the television. His hilarious clip of running back and tripping is being played on news channels repeatedly with breaking news at the bottom: Dinkar's uncle flees on seeing reporters and stumbles. What is he hiding?

Aunt and Mayank laugh out loud as Uncle switches off the TV. 'What an embarrassment this day is,' says Uncle hopelessly, as he leans back on the couch with his hands covering his face.

'Okay, now come to the dining table and eat. I am going to call Dinkar,' says Aunt, while easing the atmosphere a bit, and goes to call Dinkar from the side door. She opens the door and takes cover behind it in order to hide from the view of the reporters and cameras pointed at their house as if playing hide-and-seek.

She hollers his name from below, 'Dinkar . . . Dinkar . . . come down and eat something!'

'What have you prepared?' shouts back Dinkar.

'Khichdiii,' howls Aunt.

'Yuck! Don't want to eat hospital food!' yells Dinkar.

'Fine! Don't eat!' Aunt has no stamina today to convince him to come down and eat.

Aunt comes back in and joins her husband and son on the dining table.

'He doesn't want to eat. Let's start,' tells Aunt and begins serving them.

'Where is the curd?' asks Uncle.

'In the shop across the street. Go and fetch some?' says Aunt with a sarcastic look on her face.

Uncle gives her a cold stare and wishes he had a third eye so he could incinerate her and turn her into ash. Mayank giggles silently, like you do at someone's funeral.

As soon as they finish eating, they hear a loud banging noise, as if someone were hitting the gates with a stick. Uncle goes to check through the window. He sees two police constables standing in front of the gate. His heart starts pounding. He informs his wife and son in a shaky voice that it's the police. They too are engulfed in fear.

'Go and open! We cannot keep them waiting!' nudges Aunt as Uncle stood there like a short-term memory loss patient.

'Take the keys at least!' Aunt reminds Uncle annoyingly, as she hands him over a bunch. They lock the gates at night before going to sleep and open it in the morning, but today, due to the turn of events, they are still locked.

Uncle goes out with his legs shaking. The constable shouts as soon as he sees him, 'Ye gate kholo, sahab ayenge!' [Open the gate, our officer will visit you.] Uncle fumbles as he tries to locate the right key in the bunch. As soon as he opens the gate, two officers in plain civilian clothes alight from a car with a blue beacon on top that was waiting outside the gate. They enter the premises while the police struggle to keep the reporters at bay.

A tall well-dressed man, with black hair, grey moustache, and green aviators, greets Uncle as he extends his hand.

'Hi, I am J. P. Yadav, IPS.[Indian Police Service]. I am from NIA [National Investigation Agency]. You must be Mr Madan Chauhan,' the officer introduces himself as he shakes Uncle's hand. His grip is so tight that Uncle feels as if his hand is stuck in a sugarcane juicer. Uncle smiles in agony.

'This is Inspector Satpal Singh.' The officer introduces his subordinate. Uncle joins his hand in namaste as he is not in a position for another handshake. He watches them with apprehension as he thinks that next they will pull out handcuffs from their pocket and tell him that he is under arrest for harbouring a terrorist.

'Nothing to worry about, Chauhan sahab, let's go inside and talk,' the officer comforts him, placing his hand on Uncle's shoulder as he read the lines on his forehead. They quickly go inside as police guard their gate.

Mayank and his mother were already watching through the window. She quickly goes to her bedroom to change her dress as she is still in her nightwear. As they enter the building, Mayank greets them with folded hands and guides them to the seating area.

Both the officers, along with uncle, take their seats on the couch.

'Mr Chauhan, we are here for general enquiry. Nothing to worry. I know people become nervous on seeing us.' The officer cracks up along with his subordinate. Uncle too joins them diffidently.

After a while, Aunt comes out changed into a salwar suit with a quick face touch-up and greets the gentlemen.

'What will you have, sir?' asks Aunt.

'Tea would be fine,' replies the officer.

'Sir, actually we do not have milk as the milkman did not deliver today due to the presence of media outside. Can you please ask your people to help?' pleads Aunt as Uncle tries to hush her through hand gestures.

The officer smiles at her honesty and says, 'Sure.' He makes a call to a constable at the gate and asks Uncle to go and give him some money. Uncle goes out to the gate and hands the constable a hundred-rupee note and thanks him in advance. Meanwhile, officers inside the house ask Mayank to call Dinkar.

A few moments later, the constable returns with two packets of milk and gives to uncle. Uncle takes the milk and waits a few seconds for the constable to return the change. Too scared to ask, he just returns with the milk inside.

He hands over the milk to his wife and joins the officers on the sofa.

'We just have a few questions. I hope you will cooperate,' tells the officer.

'Sure! No problem!' says Uncle with a sigh of relief.

'Did Dinkar mention it before to you any time about being a terrorist in past life?'

'No, never. We too were equally shocked to hear that on the show,' replies Uncle.

Mayank enters and informs that Dinkar will be down shortly.

'Did makers of the show lure Dinkar into saying that?' interrogates the officer.

'No, no . . . not at all. They never tried to influence or suggest Dinkar anything any time,' Uncle dismisses the theory.

'Very well. Let me be very clear with you, Mr Chauhan. Nowadays, lots of youth make childish and unsolicited comments on matters pertaining to national security on social websites and elsewhere, and some of them even get arrested for that. Your nephew has done the same and that too on national television. Do you understand what I am saying?' explains the officer.

Uncle just regretfully nods his head in agreement.

'It hasn't gone down well with the home ministry, and they want a prompt action in this regard.' The officer is interrupted by the arrival of tea.

Aunt carries a large tray with teacups, biscuits, and namkeen (a salty, crispy snack) and serves the gentlemen. She joins the party too. Meanwhile, Dinkar also enters the hall.

'Come, Dinkar, sit!' The officer invites Dinkar in his own house in a firm voice.

Dinkar proceeds tentatively and sits there alongside Mayank with hands between his legs.

'So you attacked our parliament,' asks the officer.

Dinkar keeps quiet and looks down.

'Don't be afraid. Tell me, why did you say that on the show?'

For an Indian police officer, he appeared very kind as normally we hear that they slap first and then ask questions.

'I myself don't know. I was under hypnosis,' replies Dinkar with a choked throat.

'So do you believe that you were a terrorist in past life?'

'I don't know. I am really confused.'

'Okay. So you have no memory of your past life. Is that true?'

'Yes. Absolutely,' affirms Dinkar.

'What do you know about LeT or JeM?'

'They are terrorist organizations!' tells Dinkar.

'Have you heard of Afzal Guru?' asks the officer.

'Yes! He was sentenced to death a few years back for his role in the parliament attack!' says Dinkar.

Mayank looks at him in awe as to how he knows all this, as he is a school dropout while he himself is in college and still doesn't know that.

'And where do you know all this from?' he asks.

'I read about it on the Internet,' tells Dinkar.

Dinkar answers all questions to the officer's satisfaction. This guy is an expert human lie detector. He carefully examines Dinkar's face, voice tone, and body language as he answers his questions. He concludes that Dinkar has nothing to hide and is telling the truth.

Mayank learns that he lags far behind Dinkar in terms of general knowledge and current affairs.

'Okay, very well then. Now I was telling Mr Chauhan that you have put yourself and your family in a big soup,' the officer tries to recapitulate.

'He always does!' reacts Aunt instantly, interrupting the officer.

Dinkar gives her an indignant look, as if saying, 'Bitch!'

The officer pretends it did not happen and resumes. 'Okay. So now the situation has become very complicated. There is mounting pressure from several radical and hard-line organizations, be it Hindu or Muslim, that want Dinkar arrested. They are even planning to hold a march to demand his arrest as we speak.'

The hands and legs of all the family members turn cold.

'We, as a police department, are being very cautious in this regard because we have burnt our hands before in cases like this, as we all know that the media is a double-ended snake. If we do not arrest Dinkar, they will bite, and if we do, they will still bite. Let's face it, we will not be able to prove anything in court, and ultimately, we will become the laughing stock and punching bag for media,' the officer goes on explaining as they sip their tea.

'So now what I want you to do is that either you tell the media that the makers of the show fed that story to Dinkar or else Dinkar should admit and apologize that he was fully conscious all the time and came up with the story just to gain publicity. As he is a juvenile, we will let him go with a warning. This issue should subside as soon as possible. Do you understand what I am saying?' proposes the officer, as he repeats his stock phrase.

Uncle, Aunt, and Dinkar go into contemplation with long faces while Mayank scans his smartphone.

'Well, you don't have to answer right away. I will give you one day to decide because that's the maximum we can hold the situation from going out of hand. Inspector Satpal will liaise with you on this. Do not step out unless absolutely necessary, and do not leave the city in any case. Two constables will always be posted on your gate, day and night, till the situation subsides. Thanks for the tea!' says the officer as he gets ready to leave.

'Sir, I have something to say, if you won't mind, please!' pleads Uncle with a dead-serious face.

'Yes, go ahead,' says the officer, as everyone else wonders what Uncle is up to.

'Sir . . . that . . . that,' stammers Uncle as he finds it difficult to get his tongue to touch the right chords.

'Don't worry, Mr Chauhan, whatever it is, tell me without fear,' sympathizes the officer.

'Sir, that constable did not return the change!'

Everyone splits with laughter, including Dinkar, as Aunt slaps her head.

'I must say, Mr Chauhan, that in these trying times, you still know how to make your family laugh. I admire your attitude,' praises the officer as he bids the family goodbye.

Uncle accompanies the officers to the gate, thinking what the joke was about. He bids farewell to the officers and his fifty bucks.

Meanwhile, the aunt sharpens her canine teeth to bite Uncle as he doesn't leave any opportunity to embarrass them, especially in front of the relatives and friends due to his miserly nature. She pounces on Uncle as soon as he enters.

'Even for a few minutes, you can't put your cheap habits in your pocket. My whole life, I have suffered this humiliation time and again because of your stingy nature. All relatives and friends make fun of us. What was the need to ask change from them? He was so kind and helpful. Do you know how policemen are?' scolds Aunt.

Uncle quickly goes on the back foot to defend himself. 'But, Pushpa, it's not a matter of five or ten rupees. It's fifty rupees.' Uncle tries to explain to her the value of money.

'So what? It's fifty bucks only. I give it in tips at the beauty parlour,' boasts Aunt, but she soon realizes that she has revealed too much in zealousness.

'What?' Uncle begins to feel pain in his chest with darkness spreading in front of his eyes.

'Oho . . . it's just a figure of speech! Chill!' Aunt outwits Uncle and averts an imminent heart attack.

Chapter 12

Die, Dinkar, Die

Social media is abuzz with Dinkar Chauhan's revelation. He has become the most hated guy in the eyes of nationalists, while others brand him as a liar and attention seeker. Hindu nationalists and radicals want to see him behind bars for attacking a monument that is an icon of Indian sovereignty. The attack claimed the death of fourteen people, including six policemen.

The Muslim organizations too demand his arrest as they accuse Dinkar of lying for cheap publicity and maligning the image of Islam and its beliefs.

Dinkar is sandwiched between the two sects, as both want a piece of him.

Many jokes float on Twitter and Facebook about the episode.

Someone tweets, 'I was Dhirubhai in my past life. Can I have my Reliance back??'

Another tweets, '72 Virgins I am coming, Boom! Oh shit, wherez my thingy?'

The funny pictures on the same subject go viral too. One had Dinkar's face morphed on a skeleton lying amidst a handful of naked ladies. All the girls were wearing chastity belts. The caption read: Here are my 72 virgins!

And at the bottom left-hand corner: Mayank Chauhan and 647 others like this!

In the house, the family gathers in the seating area again to form consensus on the preferred route to take among the options given by the police officer to resolve the crisis situation that was spreading like wild fire and would soon engulf them.

Uncle suggests that it is not a good idea to put blame on the makers of the show. They all know it's not true, and sooner or later, their lie will be caught and it will lead to more embarrassment for the family. Then Aunt adds that the only way they could come out of this mess is with Dinkar's unconditional apology. Uncle and Mayank vote in favour, but Dinkar vetoes it right away as he thinks he has not done anything wrong. Uncle and Aunt try to persuade Dinkar, but we all know by now that it is futile to even try.

'Fine! Get arrested! Nobody will come to bail you out or fight for you in court,' threatens Uncle as Dinkar walks out.

The news channels begin to report about Dinkar's interrogation by the police, and some even report his arrest.

As the sun sinks below the horizon, darkness rises, not only outside but in the minds too. Uncle complains of severe headache. Apparently, the events of the day took a toll on his health. The personal blood pressure monitor registers a reading of 180/110.

Uncle panics even more on seeing the readings. Aunt calms him down and administers him a double dose of his meds as the doctor had suggested on an earlier occasion.

'Don't worry too much, ji! Take your mind off of things for some time. Have faith in God. Everything will be all right. Just lie down and rest in peace!' says Aunt as she tries to raise his spirit, probably out of the body.

'I am still alive. You say that to a dead person,' scoffs Uncle angrily as Aunt bites her tongue.

'Oh! Sorry! I mean take some rest and don't worry. I have a strong feeling that everything will be all right—'

Before she even completes that sentence, they are shaken by the ear-piercing sound of glass shattering, as Uncle looks at her with begging eyes as to why on earth she even utters this sentence. Mayank rushes to check and discovers that it was one of the front windowpanes. On closer inspection, he is horrified to find a piece of stone that was probably pelted by someone from across the road and informs his parents. The constable posted at the gate gets alarmed too and runs inside to the scene of the incident.

'What just happened?' asks the constable.

'Someone pelted stone from outside, and it smashed our window,' informs Aunt worriedly.

'Just last month only, we got it replaced,' adds the disillusioned uncle.

'I'll go and check,' tells the constable and hurries outside. He goes outside and informs his partner. One of them goes and checks around. He asks people if anyone saw anything. No one has a clue. By now the media persons too had packed up and retreated along with their crew.

The constable returns and tells the Chauhans that he could not find the culprit but assures them that they will be extra vigilant and whoever did it won't dare to repeat it again. He also tells them that if needed, the backup is not far from here. Being satisfied by the constable's assurance, they return inside.

The broken pieces of glass remind Aunt of her shattered dream. She picks the larger ones carefully by hand and dumps them in a dustbin, one by one with a shrilling heart. She murmurs to herself, 'Here goes the name, here goes the fame, here goes the praises, and here goes the envy of neighbours. Svaha!' (A Vedic exclamation used when making oblations to God.)

She sweeps the rest of the glass pieces off the floor, thinking if only there were a broom to sweep her mind off the memory of this episode of her life.

After preparing dinner, Aunt tries to convince Dinkar to come down and discuss about the serious impediment. She begs him to put aside his obstinacy and sheds a few tears in the process. Dinkar softens his stand and agrees to reassess the situation on the dinner table.

They all rush through the dinner so that a cordial solution can be reached while Dinkar is still available. They are quite familiar with his eccentric and unsettling ways. Before they could commence their small rectangular table conference, a commotion outside their gate attracts their attention. Everybody rushes to the gate with one expression, 'Now what?'

They are perturbed to see the area outside their gate swarming with people. Most of them have their heads wrapped in a saffron cloth, and they raise slogans against Dinkar and also hold placards that read: Dinkar Chauhan murdabaad (Death to Dinkar Chauhan). Mayank wishes he could join them too. The media returns to cover the protests. The constables keep calm as it is a peaceful protest. But not for long as the protestors get agitated soon and begin to pelt stones. A stone just misses Dinkar's eye, and they all run inside to take cover as in a bunker during shelling. The windows keep smashing one after the other, including the windscreen of their vintage junk. The family clings together in Aunt and Uncle's bedroom, as the drawing room is compromised with stones finding ways inside through the smashed windows.

Outside, the constables immediately request for backup over the walkie-talkie as they themselves look for shelter. The backup arrives in a few moments as they already were on high alert. The RAF (rapid action force) arrives with a truckload of personnel wearing blue camouflaged uniforms, carrying lathis (long heavy wooden sticks) and riot shields. The dissenters, small in number, disperse in no time as those lathis really hurt. Nevertheless, they hurl a few stones at the personnel, like a parting gift, as they recede into the darkness. Though some of the onlookers have to bear the brunt of lathis, and they learn it the hard way that they should mind their own business.

Inside the house, the pathetic four still lurk in fear like a bunch of mischievous kids, hiding under the bed.

Just as Uncle begins to receive visions of an impending doom, Dinkar frantically utters, 'Okay!'

'What?' asks Aunt as some hope kindles in her tone.

'Okay! I will do it!' consents Dinkar.

Aunt folds her hands and looks up towards the skies to thank God, as Uncle's BP takes a dip. As for Mayank, the adventure ride comes to a standstill. It took just one stone to bring Dinkar on line.

They come out in the hall, sensing the tornado has passed. The constables knock on the door hard with a sense of urgency to check on them if they are okay.

Uncle opens the door and tells them that they are all right. He enquires about the situation outside. One of them informs that the RAF has been deployed outside, and the crowd has dispersed. The constable himself appears more relieved than the entire family as he conveys the news to Uncle. He also advises them to stay away from the windows. As if he were Steve Jobs.

They all go to bed with prayers on their lips, wishing to wake up to a better tomorrow. As Dinkar will appear in front of the media and admit to wrongdoing, all their worries will vamoose. Aunt will place all onus on Dinkar's frail shoulders and will come out pure and pious in front of the relatives, friends, and neighbours although she is the one who drove the family to the show in her Fame Express. Uncle too will soon return to his PWD office in a day or two, where he will work less and talk more and tell stories about the incident while the files will keep piling. Mayank will resume college as Dinkar Chauhan's cousin and will enjoy the popularity because he is well aware of the fact that in college, any publicity is good publicity.

But it's poor Dinkar who will be branded as a liar tomorrow, for life. He did not do anything wrong, and he is not sure if he did anything wrong in his past life. He finds it hard to believe that he was once someone who conspired to kill others.

But then how can we forget that Dinkar is also capable of attempting suicide, and that's exactly what Aaftaab did, for a totally different reason though.

One thing that goes in Dinkar's favour is that after this fiasco will be over, he doesn't have to face anyone as he is a social outcast. He has no college to return to, no friends to answer or give justification to, and no Facebook or Twitter accounts to delete.

The next morning arrives with good written all over it. Aunt and Uncle wake up to the call of the milkman. Aunt gets out of bed and goes to the kitchen to fetch a container. She cautiously zigzags through the glass pieces and other debris lying on the floor as she steps out towards the gate. The milkman today doesn't look her in the eye as he measures 500 millilitres of milk in his cylindrical measuring cup with a twisted handle, one by one, and pours it into her steel pot through a mesh strainer. He isn't sure about the standard protocol in this situation. Would it be appropriate to enquire from her about the incidents of yesterday? Will she be comfortable to talk about it, or will he make her uneasy and offended? Well, this happens with me a lot, especially when something bad happens with a relative or friend. I am always in a muddle whether to express my sympathy with them or to just avoid touching those strings lest I play that melancholic music again that they are trying to forget. Aunt senses his dilemma and asks, 'You did not deliver yesterday?'

'I came, madam, but there were too many people outside. I got worried. Is everything all right?' he asks in a hesitant tone as he errs in calculation and delivers 500 millilitres extra in addition to the fixed 2 litres. Aunt smiles subtly as she discovers the slip and begins to tap her feet with joy.

'They were reporters who came to interview us. We appeared on a TV show, you know?'

'Yes . . . yes . . . I saw. All of you were there alongside Ravi bhaiya! Dinkar baba acted very well!' praises the milkman as Dinkar earned his one and only fan.

'Yes, indeed!' Aunt giggles at his innocence.

'But why all this mess then?' The milkman points to the broken windows.

'Side effects of becoming famous. People are just jealous,' derides Aunt.

'Very true, madam,' Agrees the milkman as if he were a celebrity before selling milk.

'You brought a smaller utensil today, madam,' informs the milkman, handing her back the pot filled with milk to the brim. Aunt smiles again, this time at his ignorance, like a con artist who just robbed his unwary victim of his most prized possession.

Soon the maid arrives too. She is most disturbed of all to see the house in such disarray and understandably so, as she is the one who has to restore order. Before she could give a presentation to Aunt on the disproportion between her salary and workload, Aunt herself picks the broom and begins to sweep. Seeing her mistress stoop to her level, she has no choice but to lend her a helping hand. Today there are neither any reporters outside the gate nor any untowardly mob. Still Aunt gets startled by something thrown inside that just lands behind her. As she turns around to check, it is today's newspaper, rolled in tight like a frankie and bent in the middle. Aunt lowers herself to pick it up as she places one hand on her creaking hackneyed knee and wails intermittently as she comes up on her feet. She straightens the newspaper up and unrolls its partially wrinkled pages. As it unfolds, the front page headlines unravel word after word.

'Protests widen as police delays Dinkar's arrest.' Below the headline is the picture of the mob in full frenzy in front of their house. Aunt quickly folds it back lest the maid sees. She hands it over to the uncle, who is eagerly awaiting its arrival, stemming the tide of his bowels. He jumps on it like a bear and rushes to relieve himself, thereafter ruining it for everybody to read. Earlier he used to read on the porch in front, but Dinkar ruined it for him.

At about 11 a.m., Inspector Satpal Singh pays them a visit to learn about their decision.

'So, Mr Chauhan, what have you decided? By the way, I tried to reach you over the phone, but it seems it is disconnected?' asks Singh as he enters the living room in his khaki uniform without cap and baton.

'Oh yes! We have disconnected because of the media. Please have a seat,' urges Uncle. Singh occupies a seat on the sofa with one leg crossed horizontally over the other, exposing the grubby sole of his shiny tan leather shoe.

'Dinkar has given his consent to appear before the media and admit his mistake,' informs Uncle.

'That is good news,' exclaims Singh as Aunt serves him a glass of cold water.

'Have a cup of tea, sir. Today we have milk,' chortles Aunt as the inspector smiles.

'Don't bother, please,' says the inspector.

'We should arrange for a press conference as early as possible because we cannot bet on Dinkar for long,' Uncle expresses his wariness.

'I will inform my superiors, and we will let you know.'

'Will Dinkar be arrested after that?' confirms Uncle.

'No,' reassures Singh.

Singh is a man of few words. They all gaze at one another for a minute, each one waiting for the other two to come up with something and break the verbal clog. Uncle is a fervid believer of the theory that neither the friendship nor the enmity with a policeman is good while Aunt knows that her tongue is like a caged anaconda, difficult to control once unleashed.

'So that's all then!' Singh gets up and takes their leave.

Dinkar has a lingering feeling of uneasiness similar to the one he used to have before the exam. He has to face a flock of journalists today. He is a book that everybody wants to read. He is the apple of the media's eye, though a rotten one. Today many a face will scowl at him, many a mouth will quiz him, and many a mind will judge him. Just to think about it sends jitters down his soul. He wants to get it over with as quickly as possible, like a person going to a dentist for extraction of a sore tooth. He begins to feel suffocated inside the four walls and decides to take a stroll in the park at noon. Even the sun laughs over his head.

Dinkar prepares to venture out, wearing a black hooded T-shirt so that he can pass inconspicuously. There is only one constable to guard the gate as the other one went for lunch. He halts Dinkar and enquires about his itinerary. Dinkar bluffs him by saying that he needs to buy some medicines as he thinks that in the absence of urgency, the constable may not allow him to go out and saunter around. It works, and the constable lets him through without surveillance as he is the only one on duty. He cautions him to be careful as he is on the punch list of many people and tells him to return right away.

Dinkar pulls the hood over his head and stretches it down over his eyes, resembling a hijab. He takes a narrow street across the road leading to the park. He clenches his nose as he passes a mound of garbage, which is probably a protected monument as it is there now for quite some time and no one dares to move it. After a few strides, he reaches a small revolving iron gate serving as one of the entrances to the park. He enters the gate and follows the uneven walkway laid with stepping stones. He hates them as he finds it difficult to synchronize his steps with the spacing of stones. It annoys him when he lands his foot in between the stones on the soft ground as if he lost a life in a video game and should start over. It leads him to his favourite vantage point, a wooden bench. There is nothing to gaze at except the greenery and the deserted swings and slides as people are scared to catch a tan in this part of the world.

As he sits there for a few minutes, an abridged version of his whole (but far from wholesome) life begins to play in front of his eyes on the curtain of green grass. He ponders if this journey called life is worth the struggle, fear, uncertainties, enigma, dejection, and misery that one has to endure while on the way to a common destination called death. What is life after all? Was he really Aaftaab, or was it just a devilry of his unconscious mind? Why does it bother people anyway? Why do they want him punished so badly? Isn't this life a punishment enough?

Amid these thoughts, someone hits Dinkar on the head from behind, and he falls unconscious.

The constable begins to worry as half an hour passes without Dinkar's reversion. His throat dries up with panic as fifteen more precious minutes pass uneventfully. He knows he has put himself and his job in jeopardy. The chances are meagre, but the optimist in him suggests that Dinkar may have slipped inside unnoticed, and he should check inside before raising the alarm. He rings the bell on the gate, and Aunt appears shortly. He requests a refill on his water bottle from the aunt. She soon returns holding the chilled bottle with condensate droplets sliding down its face, similar to that of the constable's face. He enquires from the aunt if everyone is doing fine inside the house. She confirms that everyone is doing fine. He does not get what he is looking for, so he refabricates his question. 'Did everyone sleep well last night?'

'Yes, we did! Thanks to you! Dinkar might still be sleeping. He wakes till late at night and sleeps until noon. I should go and check on him,' says Aunt as she prepares her knees to climb the stairs.

A delinquent idea begins to float over the constable's mind on the account of information received from the aunt. What if he doesn't tell anyone that Dinkar sneaked out? There was no one present at the gate except him when Dinkar left. There aren't any CCTVs in the vicinity, and to top it all, the family is unaware too. If he is questioned later about Dinkar's disappearance, he can firmly state that he was guarding the entrance the entire time, and there was no chance Dinkar could go unchecked. Dinkar could have easily strayed through the intricate network of intertwined roofs. If Dinkar returns later and tries to sell him out, his story can be easily dismissed as another figment of his imagination like the rest doing rounds in the country. He thinks it through like Sherlock Holmes. He may manage to save his job but not his integrity.

Aunt climbs up to the first floor only to discover that Dinkar is not in his room. She hollers to her husband to check if Dinkar is down. Uncle confirms the opposite. She treks to the summit of the building to look for Dinkar. But he is nowhere to be found, bringing their worst fears to life. They inform the constable at last that they are not able to locate Dinkar. The constable had foreseen it already but feigns a shock. He conducts a mock search with them and advises them to check the washrooms while wasting precious time. Once sure about Dinkar's disappearance, the constable radios the message to the police station about Dinkar's vanishing act.

The news bounces off someone's slippery tongue and tosses into the media. It becomes breaking news on every saleable channel and an embarrassment for the police.

'Dinkar vanishes under the nose of the police.'

'Dinkar, missing or absconding? Police and family don't have a clue.'

Media throng their gate again as police teams undertake a frantic search to locate Dinkar. He doesn't carry a mobile phone, so his last known location is based purely on visual perception of the human eye rather than the electromagnetic signals from any mobile tower. To the constable's amusement, his last reported appearance is on the previous night, and he could be anywhere by now. Uncle and Aunt learn that their woes are far from getting over today. They still attend the press conference and blame Dinkar for all their afflictions and save their asses.

Chapter 13

Welcome to Paradise

Dinkar regains consciousness and discovers that he is an entity without a physical body. He is just a self-aware globule of thoughts, floating in space with no sense of direction or purpose as he glistens with divine light. He concludes that he is dead and his spiritual journey has begun through the astral plane. He is devoid of fear, anger, hate, lust, and other earthly emotions and bristles with serenity. Well, he has always been free from lust. The feeling that blooms in him is impossible to define in words for it's non-existent in the physical world. Calling it bliss would be like calling Taj Mahal a graveyard.

Then out of nowhere, a black thunderous cloud wearing a treacherous face drifts over him and eclipses the divine light while hailing the dark forces to rise from their slumber. As it casts a shadow on Dinkar's consciousness, he abruptly transcends into his astral body. The next moment, he finds himself lying on a hot stony arid planet, wearing nothing except his bewilderment. Its surface is perforated with volcanic fissures as far as the vision goes. The fissures spew a scintillating yet pungent dark green gas that sporadically fizzes out into the dark sky as if there lies a dragon underneath the surface. Without notice, the fissures cease to erupt as if someone closed their valves all at once. And if it wasn't macabre enough for Dinkar, tiny black serpents begin to ooze out of the orifices, as if released from a confinement, and crawl towards him. The gravity on the planet appears to be ten times more than that on earth because Dinkar finds himself shackled to the surface as he watches the serpents advance. They converge at him from all directions like he was their Mecca. Each of the slimy creatures enters his body, percolating through his skin, as if returning home. He feels ticklish at first, but as more and more of them take sanctuary inside his body, it becomes excruciatingly painful. All the earthly emotions begin to thrive in him again and darkness takes him over.

He wakes up completely wasted and finds himself imprisoned in his physical body. His sense of smell, touch, and hearing work fine, but taste and sight dwindle, as he feels paralyzed, unable to move a muscle. Probably he was injected with some kind of drug. So it was all just a dream then, he broods over, or was it? He will never know for sure. Be it a memory of a past event or a dream, it lodges in our brain without prejudice. After subsequent time has lapsed, you cannot distinguish which one was real and which was fake. Sometimes the dreams are more palpable than the reality. Sometimes the reality appears more specious than a dream.

Dinkar can hear two men chattering close by. He wants to get up as he has to pee but has no control over his limbs. Fortunately, he has control over his bladder. Soon his mind regains full control over his body, and he slowly lifts up his eyelids. A lofty lined wooden ceiling watches over him.

Either the ceiling was sloping inwards or his vision had concaved. A face, covered partially in short white beard, blocks his view of the ceiling.

'Welcome to the paradise!' greets the old man wearing a white rounded skullcap.

Really! An old man welcoming me to paradise? Where are all the hoories *or apsaras [native female inhabitants of heaven]?* Dinkar thinks to himself. *So I really am dead!*

He gets out of the sag of the knotted bed with considerable effort assisted by the old man. The floor, planked with wood, squeaks with every step he takes with his bare feet as he reaches out for a small window across the room. He takes a peek outside, and the view blows away his senses.

It's a valley painted in green, orange, red, and yellow, resembling an assorted bouquet. The maple leaves embellish every inch of the ground in preparation of welcoming winter. The snow-clad peaks goggle over the tall chinar trees, as if standing on their toes and stretching high to catch a glimpse of Dinkar. His namesake has just risen the same time as him. Its inclined rays light up the dewdrops on the leaves like a million LEDs dancing on the night of Diwali. The tranquillity of the wilderness is such that Dinkar can hear his heart beating in admiration, as if his whole life, he were in pursuit of this place. It's paradise indeed.

'What place is this?' asks Dinkar.

'Kashmir,' declares the old man with a sense of pride in his tremulous voice.

The fourth Mogul emperor, Jahangir, was so mesmerized with its natural glamour that he recited a couplet in Persian:

Gar Firdaus bar roo-e zameen ast,

Hameen asto, hameen asto, hameen ast!

If there is paradise on earth,

It's here, it's here, it's here.

Evidently, Jahangir had not been to Switzerland, and neither has Dinkar. But I have been, and believe you me, the couplet still holds good after 400 years. Dinkar is so awestruck by his surroundings it doesn't bother him that he is being held as a captive. He doesn't care about their identity or their intentions.

Dinkar is held in a small sequestered, frayed hut carved completely out of wood, raised a couple of feet above the ground on wood posts on a sloping mountain in the wild.

Once he gets the hang of reality, he discovers that he is wearing a black and white chequered pheran (a loose gown with long sleeves worn by Kashmiri men and women) over his clothes, as is the old man. It's chilly compared to Delhi, but the pheran keeps him warm. He asks the old man for directions to the washroom as he hasn't relieved himself in twenty hours. The elderly man points him to a door. Dinkar hastens towards it, as if it were the door of a train leaving the platform. He pulls it open and is baffled to learn that it leads outside via a wooden staircase. He turns around and shrugs his shoulders at the old man, as if he were a prankster from *Betty White's Off Their Rockers.* The man again gestures by extending his arm in the direction of door, as if telling him, 'Go on, son! Find a sweet spot under the sky, dig a little hole, and relieve yourself of all your bothering while enjoying the view. The whole world is your toilet!'

The old man hands him a bucket of water and accompanies him, carrying a double-barrelled gun so that he can watch him. Not watch him defecate but keep a lookout in case he tries to escape. I say just take his clothes and he will be too ashamed to escape. But Dinkar has no plans to disappear any more. He already escaped from what he dreaded the most. He cannot thank his kidnappers enough for bringing him here. Besides, he could not run even if he wanted to as he is too exhausted.

Dinkar does not want to smear the heavenly beauty of the landscape. It's something to be revered, not crap upon. It's like going to the Louvre and spitting on Mona Lisa while chewing gutkha, or tobacco. But you gotta do what you gotta do.

After attending to nature's call, Dinkar is served with kahwa, or Kashmiri green tea. He holds the mug clenched between the palms of his hands in order to conduct some heat. The old man gawks at him as if waiting for him to take a sip.

'How is it?' he asks Dinkar for a review like a professional chef as soon as he tastes some.

'Good! Thank you!' tells Dinkar, which puts a smile on his parched, reddened face.

He does not like the taste but follows the decorum of a good captive and drinks it anyway, as the old man is not his aunt and he also has a gun.

Something bothers him as he pulls out some strands sticking to his tongue.

'That's saffron! The most expensive spice in the world. It'll boost your virility,' the old man enlightens Dinkar.

Dinkar immediately swallows them as he badly needs some because he has suffered an erectile dysfunction in the past. He admires his hospitality as his aunt used to keep two sets of tea leaves, an expensive one for the family and a cheaper one for the unwanted guests.

A sudden reminiscence hits him. He heard two people in his semi-conscious state. He sees only one. It's highly unlikely that the old man brought him there all the way from Delhi. Soon his doubts vanish as another man in his late thirties, exhibiting a grey beard without a moustache, enters through the door without knocking. He carries an AK rifle in one hand and food in another. Dinkar feels intimidated by his presence.

He introduces himself right away. 'I am Ikhlaq.'

'Dinkar,' he introduces back while observing a deep scar carefully concealed under his beard.

He asks the man tentatively, 'Why have you brought me here?'

'Soon you will come to know,' says Ikhlaq with a sigh.

It fuels his fretfulness. But then Dinkar thinks, *What the heck, just look at the landscape outside.* Even if he dies here, he will have no regret. It's a fair bargain. Anything is better than returning to Delhi and facing the media. He overhears the two men chatting and comes to know that they are a father–son duo as Ikhlaq addresses him as Abbu.

Like a complimentary lunch on a honeymoon package, Dinkar is offered lamb curry and rice in the afternoon. He has always had that chronic craving for meat while living with his aunt and uncle that mostly went unassuaged. He feasts on the lamb while enjoying the pristine view. This is by far the best meal of his life. He spends the rest of the day gaping at the trees in disquietude. In the evening, the sky dons the colour of the orange maple trees as the sun begins its downward leap. Dinkar sleeps on his charpoy while the two prepare their bed on the wooden floor by spreading blankets.

Two days pass by, and Dinkar begins to feel restless as they do not give him any information about his fate. But he is happy as long as they serve him tasty non-vegetarian food. Tonight all his questions are going to be answered.

As the night is in its full bloom, he notices Ikhlaq preparing a backpack, loading some gadgets, batteries, a torchlight, some food, water, and warm clothing as if going on a hiking trip. He also packs a couple of magazines, not to read but to reload his rifle with, if required. Dinkar watches him in consternation. He hands over a winter jacket, a monkey cap, a pair of woollen socks, and shoes to Dinkar to wear as the journey they are going to embark upon would be uncomfortable in a pheran. Dinkar gets into them without questioning and just receives his fate with open hands.

Dinkar bids goodbye to the old man and thanks him for his hospitality as he bends down to touch his feet. The old man quickly recedes back and tells him that they don't touch feet here. He hugs him instead and says, 'Khuda hafiz [Lord be your protector].'

Ikhlaq and Dinkar set out in the dark on foot. For Dinkar, the darkness is literal as well as figurative, as he is unaware of the destination. Ikhlaq ties a rope around Dinkar's waist and carries the other end in his hand. He leads the way as if grazing his goat. It's for Dinkar's own safety so that he doesn't stray in the dark and be chewed up by a nocturnal carnivore. Fortunately for Dinkar, the air is unstirred, or it would have been very cold. The moon is on leave today, and the visibility is a few metres under the stars. They walk uphill without any trail through the grass and bushes. The bushes often entangle in Dinkar's feet as if begging not to proceed further. The cricket's chirp, and distant howls of hyenas add to the ghostly ambience of the savage jungle. Dinkar wonders, *What did Ikhlaq bring the torchlight for?* Some slopes are steeper than the others, and Ikhlaq has to grab on to bushes and shrubs in order to climb. Then he pulls Dinkar up as he holds on to the rope. After dragging him for forty-five minutes straight, they reach the crest of the hill. Dinkar finally gets a view of some civilization after two days in the form of a distant cluster of lights on the other side of the valley. It's like viewing another galaxy through an astronomical telescope. A narrow noisy river meanders through the rift below. They rest for a while on the grass to grab some breath. The hike exhausts Dinkar completely as he is not used to long gravity-defying walks. Ikhlaq gives him water and food to replenish his energy.

'Do you see those lights?' asks Ikhlaq.

'Duh! I am not blind!' Dinkar wanted to answer but instead just settles for, 'Yes', as he bites on the roti rolls stuffed with kababs. It's like a midnight picnic for Dinkar.

'It's PoK,' tells Ikhlaq.

'Really,' Dinkar utters in a daze. 'You mean Pakistan-occupied Kashmir?' confirms Dinkar.

'Yes. Azad Kashmir,' tells Ikhlaq in a nostalgic voice. Ikhlaq and his father, Abdul, were once the natives of Muzaffarabad, capital of PoK, but many years back, they crossed the Line of Control to enter into Indian territory so they could build up the local infrastructure to help the passing infiltrators with the supplies and support.

'And that must be Jhelum?' asks Dinkar, pointing to the river, boasting his general knowledge.

'No. It's Kishanganga, or Neelum as it's known on the other side. It merges into Jhelum a few hundred kilometres downstream,' lectures Ikhlaq, as he ameliorates his general knowledge

The river, also binomial like Dinkar, unwillingly divides the two lands, amicable as a community but hostile as a nation.

'When the time is right, we will cross the river,' informs Ikhlaq. Dinkar's heart begins to knock on his chest. His mind begins to make all sorts of assumptions. Maybe the people belonging to the terrorist outfit want to punish him themselves for making up Aaftaab.

'But why?' he asks Ikhlaq.

'I don't know. I am just the delivery boy,' tells Ikhlaq.

His doubts begin to realize. And the roaring of the river alone makes his legs shudder, forget about crossing it.

'But I don't know how to swim,' he tries to fit in an excuse.

'Don't worry, I know a shallow route. Just hold on to my hand, and you will be fine,' tells Ikhlaq like an expert.

Sensing no way out, he grabs on to the grass and the soil underneath in both his fists tightly, as if bidding farewell to his beloved homeland. The vision of his house, Uncle, and Aunt whirl in front of him. He had a faint hope that kindled deep down in his heart of returning home someday in the future when the healing hands of time would excise the memory of the incident from the minds of the people, but now he knows he is at the point of no return. Even his body won't find a way back. The inevitable fact makes him distraught. He goes mute and awaits further orders from his guide.

Chapter 14

A Diwali of Sorts

Ikhlaq scouts the area through his night-vision binoculars. The area had few Indian watchtowers and that too far away. Then he opens the bag and pulls out a satellite phone. He transmits a short coded message and hangs up. After half an hour or so, Ikhlaq pokes Dinkar as he had dozed off. It is time to start their descent of the hill to the river. Ikhlaq gathers his stuff, and they begin to climb down.

On the way, they come across a deserted village whose inhabitants must have fled due to rampant firing in this area. They jump through the abandoned step fields, which once used to thrive under peaceful conditions. They reach the foot of the mountain fairly quickly, jumping and sliding down, like kids in a Mickey Mouse jumping castle, while hiding from the watch posts at the same time. On reaching the wide open shores of the river, a wire fencing welcomes them. It stands just a few hundred metres away, built to deter infiltrators such as themselves.

'Now what? We cut through the wires?' asks Dinkar, exasperated from the journey.

Ikhlaq sniggers as he bends down and begins to clear the ground of stones and sand. A large wooden cover similar to that of a manhole begins to surface as he removes more sand and stones. Dinkar peers at it in amazement while Ikhlaq removes the cover. There appears a dark hole beneath, wide enough for two people to fit in standing abreast. Ikhlaq asks him to jump inside the hole. It's as if one of his many suicide ideas managed to transpire in reality, to jump in a black hole and get crushed under its boundless gravity. He dreads the idea lest Ikhlaq puts back the lid and cover it again with sand and stones, turning it into his living grave. He refuses at once. Ikhlaq jumps inside with his rifle on the shoulder without wasting any more time as they are on a tight schedule. The pit isn't deep enough as Ikhlaq's head still bulges out of the ground. Near the bottom of the trench, a small horizontal tunnel opens into it, wide and high enough for a single person to crawl. He asks Dinkar to pass on his backpack. Dinkar hands him the backpack, and Ikhlaq throws it inside the tunnel after taking out a couple of flashlights. Then he asks Dinkar to enter. Sensing the depth of the pit and with Ikhlaq there to assist him, Dinkar jumps in too. They are crammed in that congested space abreast each other, trying hard to keep their loins from touching, like two guys doing a paper dance. Ikhlaq asks him to bend his knees as he pulls the cover over their head, and it goes completely dark without a single photon of light. Ikhlaq struggles to switch on the flashlight while Dinkar begins to panic. After three or four rapid spanks at its bottom, the flashlight switches on, and their faces light up like ghostly apparitions. Ikhlaq hands another flashlight to Dinkar and crawls into the tunnel, showing the way to

Dinkar as he keeps pushing his backpack in front of him. Dinkar crawls behind him as the ants and other insects keep him company and race with him. It's a living hell for Dinkar as he hates insects. We all do. After crawling for about 200 metres, they emerge out on the other side of the fence. The river flows in front of them and appears more treacherous from such close proximity.

'Why didn't you use the torch in the jungle? It was so dark up there,' grumbles Dinkar.

'If I did that, we would have been dead by now. You cannot give your position away to the BSF [Border Security Force],' tells Ikhlaq as he grinds his teeth. 'Why else do you think we crossed on a no-moon night?' He pulls out his satellite phone and makes another call. He tells the person on the other side in Urdu that they are ready. He takes shelter behind a large stone along with Dinkar. Suddenly the rangers across the LoC open fire as Dinkar clings on to Ikhlaq. The flickering streaks of light emanate from the other side of the valley. As the bullets strike the mountains above them, sparks fly just like crackers on Diwali.

It is a Diwali of sorts. On that day, Lord Ram returned to Ayodhya (along with his wife, Sita, and brother, Lakshman) after living in exile for fourteen years. Dinkar, alias Aaftaab, is also going to return home after living in exile for seventeen years. People of Ayodhya lit diyas, or oil lamps, to commemorate Lord Ram's return, as it was an Amavasya, or no-moon night. Aaftaab is being welcomed by firing from Pakistani rangers, and this too is a no-moon night. Lord Ram was helped by Hanuman, while Aaftaab has Ikhlaq to show him the way. The similarities are remarkable, though

Dinkar stands nowhere close to Lord Ram, as he was the pinnacle of morality and virtue, and neither does Ikhlaq possess the loyalty, devotion, and selfless service of Lord Hanuman.

'Don't worry, that's our cover,' tells Ikhlaq. 'Hold on to my hand. Let's go.' Dinkar grabs his hand tightly.

He enters into the waist-deep icy cold water of Kishanganga, aka Neelum, as Dinkar follows him, holding his hand as if performing the Kashmiri folk dance. The water occasionally reaches their chest as it jumps over the stones that act as flow breakers. It requires a great deal of effort, especially by Dinkar, to hold himself against the vigorous flow of the river. He is like a tree in the tempest. If it were not for Ikhlaq, Dinkar would have been washed away in a blink. Ikhlaq knows every inch of the riverbed and the location of stones to stick his feet against in order to ride out the flow. Dinkar almost loses his balance as his foot slips over a slimy stone, but he latches on to Ikhlaq's arm as he helps him regain posture. They finally cross to the opposite side, fully drenched, and quickly take cover as the firing begins from the Indian side too. Ikhlaq asks him to lose the wet clothing and change into the ones he packed, as he does the same, to avoid catching a cold or even hypothermia. He makes another call to inform his contacts that they are through. There aren't any fences on this side of the LoC.

The firing fades away after some time and then halts completely. Dinkar quivers badly, like a dashboard doll in a moving car, and his feet hurt as the chill drills through his bones. He has undergone a rigorous commando routine tonight, beginning with traversing a mountain, crawling into the tunnel, crossing an obstinate river, and finally taking cover under fire. But he has to undergo a last routine, and the most formidable of all, the rock climbing. Ikhlaq receives a call on his phone, following which he prepares to proceed forward. He helps Dinkar get on his feet, and they follow a path uphill. This strenuous exercise warms up Dinkar as he feels heat flowing in his body again. After walking for another hour and elevating a few hundred feet, they reach an escarpment beyond which they have to climb via ropes. The rope along with harness lay in wait at the rendezvous position. Ikhlaq helps Dinkar tie the harness while Dinkar thanks the heavens as he doesn't have to walk any more. Once the harness is secured on Dinkar's body, Ikhlaq bids him goodbye, still holding the rope tied to Dinkar. He has delivered his package successfully. Dinkar is mournful as well as frightened to learn that Ikhlaq will not accompany him any further and he will be completely at the mercy of people above. Ikhlaq has been very kind and he thanks him for that. Ikhlaq signals his counterparts above as he flashes to them. Dinkar waves at him, afflicted with grief, as he is heaved up slowly through a winch on a mini truck. Ikhlaq monitors him from below as he steadies his ascent, holding the rope until he is in safe hands.

Two decent-looking armed men, wearing pathani suits and jackets, on top pull him up. After untying the harness and detaching the ropes, they ask Dinkar to hop in front with them. They begin their road trip on a menacing curly road full of potholes and sharp bends that unfold like a mystery novel gradually under the headlights, with an overhanging mountain on the right and a steep gorge on the left. At some places, the road is so narrow that it's difficult for two vehicles to pass alongside unless they are two-wheelers. Now it is the turn of Indian Kashmir to showcase its glitter on the black canvas of the night on the other side of the valley.

He feels at home as they speak Punjabi, which is widely spoken in parts of Delhi as well as in his own house. The bumpy ride, synonymous with that of a roller coaster, makes Dinkar throw up. Fortunately, he occupies a window seat. The gentlemen seem supportive as they advise him to close his eyes and lie back. Even the rumbling of a diesel engine falls as lullaby on the ears of a fatigued person such as Dinkar, and he soon falls asleep.

He wakes up after a few hours when the tempo halts and engines go silent. It halts in front of a guest house on a gradient. It takes a minute or two for Dinkar to adjust to the brightness of the day as he opens his eyes. All three of them alight and proceed inside. The view is equally awesome from here, but Dinkar doesn't care and just needs a bed to crash. Soon he is shown a room with a single occupancy, and he does not waste any time to lose extra clothing and slides under a blanket. He sleeps till noon and wakes on his own. It's such an achievement when you wake all by yourself without an alarm or a doorbell or a splash of water, having a fair share of your sleep. He is a bit surprised though that no one came to check on him. He steps out of his room and finds a man wearing a safa guarding his door.

'Assalam-u-alaikum [Peace be unto you],' he greets.

'Wa-alaikum-salam [And unto you peace].' Dinkar knows the standard reply.

'Kuch kaayega? [Want to eat something?]' he asks. He appears Pathan by his accent.

'In a while.' Dinkar smiles.

'Let me know,' he tells Dinkar.

No one seems to be in a hurry here, unlike his aunt who pestered him his whole life only to come down and eat.

He steps out in the balcony of his room and douses in the pulchritude of his surroundings. The guest house is situated on a mountain slope overlooking a large city that lies in prostration before the majestic mountains all around, which in return bless it with not one but two rivers. The rivers zigzag through the city before amalgamating. For an ignorant eye, it's difficult to infer as to whether they part ways or form a union. To a pessimist, it will appear as if the cruel hands of nature sliced the river in half, like a person being lynched with his arms stretched in opposite directions. To an optimist, it would appear to be a fusion of two lovers aided by the divine interception, as if someone weaves two twigs into one. It is the city of Muzaffarabad, the parallel of Srinagar.

Dinkar takes a long hot shower after a gap of three days. A new set of clothes lies waiting on his bed. After getting ready, the Pathan guides him to the mess for lunch. He orders lamb curry and roti of which he has grown fond of recently. It's even tastier than one he had on the Indian side. The aroma is exquisite, and he gets its taste before he could take a bite. As he enjoys his food, many men ogle over his smooth face and slender body. He gets uncomfortable and goes about swallowing the rest of it. After lunch, the Pathan takes him out in the guest house's private garden. A bald, middle-aged, slightly healthy man with a bushy moustache occupies a chair in the centre with his head tilted back in contemplation, surrounded by four armed bodyguards. He appears a big shot, probably a local politician or a larger-than-life Bollywood villain.

'Assalam-u-alaikum bhaijaan?' greets the Pathan.

The man opens his eyes and looks over his nose to check who it is. 'Wa-alaikum-salam Bashir,' he greets back as he lifts his head.

Bashir presents Dinkar to him and takes his leave. The man gestures to his armed guards to leave the two of them alone.

'So Aaftaab! I hope you had a comfortable ride,' he enquires.

Dinkar just nods in agreement.

'My name is Altaaf. Does it ring a bell?' he asks in a condescending tone.

Dinkar shakes his head in negative.

'You say you are Aaftaab, and you don't recognize your older brother?' asks Altaaf with derision as he stands off the chair.

Dinkar is flabbergasted. He cannot believe his ears as well as his eyes. How is this possible? How could a harvest of his imagination realize. Until now he doubted his existence and thought he made him up, but now his brother stands right in front of him. Just when he reconciles with the fact that Aaftaab is his own creation, idea of his existence is thrown to his face.

'I really don't know any more. Who am I?' expresses helpless Dinkar, surrendering himself to his dual identity.

'I know! You are not Aaftaab, as he is in paradise, enjoying the fruits of his martyrdom,' Altaaf says, exalting Aaftaab.

'So why have you brought me here?' asks Dinkar. His heart rate elevates as his life depends upon the answer to this question.

'To fulfil a mother's dying wish,' says Altaaf with a sigh while folding his arms.

'Whose mother?' asks Dinkar.

'Aaftaab's mother. My mother. And now yours too,' says Altaaf, as if offering a contract.

'She has been asking to see Aaftaab one last time before she dies as she thinks he is imprisoned in India. Nothing can console a mother's heart who lost her son so young except the son himself. Then someone told me about you. I don't want to say it, but your resemblance to Aaftaab is striking!' tells Altaaf as he hands him over an old crinkly postcard-size picture of Aaftaab from the pocket of his pathani suit. Dinkar holds the picture with trembling hands. He is startled to notice the uncanny resemblance except that he had longer hair. He had the same doleful eyes as that of Dinkar. Could this all be a coincidence? Dinkar meditates. If Dennis the Menace could be conceived by two minds working independently at the same time on different sides of the globe, then this comparatively is less bizarre.

'So what do you want me to do?' asks Dinkar naively.

'Just pretend to be Aaftaab, like you have been doing so far,' says Altaaf sarcastically, pouring acid on his wounds.

Dinkar doesn't have the luxury of another option and accepts his dictates. He wants to ask him about his alternatives in case the old woman dies, but he doesn't want to sound impudent and get shot in the head.

'You'll get everything you need. Just remember that you are my brother, Aaftaab, only in my house, for outsiders, you are just a distant relative,' Altaaf explains him the salient points of the agreement. Dinkar is briefed thoroughly by Altaaf about his new assignment.

Chapter 15

The Beautiful Interpreter

Altaaf and Dinkar leave the guest house along with his men in a convoy for a place which Dinkar believes is going to be his home for the rest of his life. It's a few kilometres uphill on the same road. The road is comparatively level and wide. The cars halt in front of a small round gate covered with flowering shrubs, like that of a banquet hall decorated for welcoming a *baraat*, or a wedding procession. The gate opens to a series of stone steps leading to an old but well-maintained red bungalow with green corrugated sloping tin roofs, with a garden upfront but a few steps lower than the building as it's built on a slope. The garden is wide enough for children to play cricket as it's an unending struggle to find an open space, flat and wide enough for playing cricket in hill stations. But there are no children in this house. As Dinkar scales the steps behind Altaaf, he suffers from stage fright, like an actor on his maiden performance. The sight of the colourful garden blooming with roses and their sweet fragrance eases him a bit as he takes a deep breath.

Upon entering the house, Dinkar feels as if he has entered a museum. The living area is stuffed with antiques like a gramophone, sand clocks that ran out of sand, the phone with a dial, and decorated earthenware. The wooden ceiling exhibits beautiful limned designs. The seating area is covered with Kashmiri carpet, and sofas resemble a sultan's throne. There is a fireplace in the living room, and above it, the wall displays a head of a barasingha, while the adjacent wall is covered with the hide of a tiger. The wall opposite to it boasts of two antique guns hanging in an *X* form. It appears as if it's a family of hunters or mercenaries.

There is a young lady with her back turned towards them, sitting on a chair in a corner. She wears a yellow embroidered palazzo suit, and her head is partially draped with her dupatta as she works on her laptop.

'Arisha', cries Altaaf, 'meet Aaftaab.'

She is startled by the sudden entry of her father as if she were surfing porn (which she wasn't). She shuts the laptop lid and covers her head fully as she gets up and turns around to meet his reincarnated uncle.

'Khushamdeed [Welcome],' she greets blushingly.

Dinkar just bows his head, blushing twice as more as he catches her one glimpse. Arisha is a gorgeous young woman, around the same age as Dinkar. He hasn't seen anyone so beautiful standing so close to him in his entire life. Jahanvi would appear an ape in front of her. Her skin is not just white but rosy white, like that of a baby who has yet to see sunlight. Her eyes are green as if studded with emerald and features so sharp that it would slit anyone's heart from the first sight. She has a perfect body and height, which could easily win her a beauty pageant, but such events are still a taboo and are widely regarded as degrading for women here.

'She will be your interpreter as my mother speaks only Punjabi. Our family hails from Rawalpindi,' tells Altaaf. Arisha too is aware of what's going to cook in her house.

Dinkar wants to inform him that he understands Punjabi well, but he wasn't a fool any more so as to refuse the services of such a beautiful interpreter.

It's time to visit the mother. She is bedridden in an adjacent room. She doesn't have any life-threatening condition but a little bit of everything, like type 2 diabetes, hypertension, rheumatoid arthritis, and above all, delusions. There is a full-time nurse to take care of her.

All three enter the room that resembles a hospital ward with a single bed. An old woman, though of sturdy construction, lies on the bed, sighing while a nurse sits by her side, reading a book. Alongside the bed lie a saline stand and a folded wheelchair. For a woman in her seventies, she looks quite plump. Her skin has sagged like her morale but is still unwrinkled. Her knees are done too supporting her weight. Altaaf signals the nurse to leave the room.

'See, Ammi, who has come,' says Altaaf, as he joggles her arm.

She opens her eyes and sees a faint apparition of three people of which she is familiar with the two. The images become clear as Altaaf helps her put on her glasses kept on the side table.

'Aaftaab, my son,' she cries at once as she sees Dinkar and sees her lost son in him. She asks him to come near her, extending her hand. Dinkar proceeds further hesitantly.

She grabs his hand with both her hands so that he doesn't run away again and sobs while placing his hand on her eyes and then kisses it vehemently as Dinkar sits by her side. It's the first time in his living memory that someone treated him with so much affection and love. He feels an unknown warmth in his heart. Altaaf and Arisha console her as everything is going to be fine again.

'See how frail you have become? The Indians did not feed you?' she says in Punjabi as Arisha and Altaaf chuckle, and Dinkar plays dumb and smiles.

'She is saying that you have become very weak,' tells Altaaf.

For Aaftaab's mother, Dinkar is the same Aaftaab that left her seventeen years ago. Her delirious brain has taken her seventeen years back in time. She is still living in 2001. As Aaftaab left in his twenties but returned a teenager, she thinks he has lost weight as he was starved in an Indian prison. She doesn't recognize her granddaughter, Arisha, as for her she is just a one-year-old kid. She often refers to Arisha as 'that girl who stays in our house'.

'I have seen a girl for you. Soon we'll get you married. Do you like this girl?' she asks Dinkar while aiming at Arisha.

'You take rest, Ammi. Aaftaab isn't going anywhere now,' fumes Altaaf over her indecent proposal. Arisha splits into laughter and runs out of the room. As for Dinkar, *yes* was dancing on his tongue. Altaaf thinks Dinkar did not understand so there was no need to explain to him. Soon they both leave her with her delusions and nurse. It's time for her afternoon nap.

151

They come out in the living room and get seated in the dining area. Altaaf devours his lunch as he is in a hurry. Altaaf tells Dinkar that he will send a tailor in the evening to take his measurements in order to stitch some clothes for him. He tells their maid, Saqina to prepare Aaftaab's room and leaves with his men. All the rooms are on the same level adjacent to one another as the building is a single-storey.

'Did you take lunch, Aaftaab chachu [uncle who is father's brother]?' asks Arisha teasingly.

'Yes, I did, in the guest house. Thank you!' tells Dinkar slightly abashed. 'What about you?'

'Already,' she says. 'So Abbu told me you are an Indian.'

'Yes. You don't get Indian channels here?' he asks.

'Not in this house. I don't know how he allowed you inside, otherwise everything that's Indian is banned in here,' mutters Arisha as she confides to Dinkar.

Dinkar feels a little relieved to know that Arisha does not know about his past and, hence, doesn't have a preconceived opinion about him.

'Tell me about India. How is life there?' asks Arisha curiously.

'Same as here. But here, girls are more beautiful,' tells Dinkar.

Arisha laughs out loud. She is amused as well as flattered by his innocence. 'How many have you seen?' she enquires.

'Many!' he tells her.

'Really! Where?' she asks with bewilderment.

'On TV, during a cricket match in Lahore,' he says playfully as her expressions begin to change.

She looks at him with indignation as she thought all this while he was referring to her. Dinkar soon senses displeasure on her face and tries to mend fences.

'But they too were nothing compared to you.' He puts back a smile on her face right where he stole and a little blush too.

It's a beginning of a seemingly incestuous, one-sided affair for Dinkar, but in reality, they are not even remotely related. Dinkar thanks God a hundred times at least, for bringing him here. He feels as if he always belonged here. A beautiful place, a beautiful house, and beautiful people, what more can one ask for?

Arisha tells Dinkar that if he needs anything, he can ask Saqina, as she will be busy on her laptop with her college project.

In the evening, when the old lady wakes up, she asks for Aaftaab. The nurse informs Arisha. Arisha goes looking for Dinkar outside as he strolls in their garden.

'Seems like you are an admirer of nature,' says Arisha, as she tries to catch up with him from behind.

Dinkar halts and turns around. 'Yes, I am,' he replies, as his eyes glow at her sight.

'Badi Ammi has asked for you, chachu!' Arisha mocks him again, calling him uncle as he looks even younger to her. Arisha addresses her grandmother as badi ammi.

'Please don't call me that. You know I am not him,' begs Dinkar.

'Are you sure?' she asks.

Dinkar pauses for a while and replies, 'No.'

'So when you are sure, let me know. I'll stop addressing you as chachu,' tells Arisha, giggling.

'I am sure. I am sure,' reacts Dinkar quickly.

Arisha guffaws as if she had called his bluff while Dinkar just bows his head in discomfiture, partly embarrassed by himself and partly due to her dupatta sliding off her chest. She quickly gathers and drapes it all over and pretends like nothing happened.

They go inside and appear before the old lady. She asks Dinkar if he has eaten anything at all. Arisha confirms that he already did. The old lady scorns at Arisha as if she were a servant and asks her to let Aaftaab reply. Arisha doesn't feel bad as she understands her condition and enjoys it as a comedy. She tries to suppress her laughter and whispers to Dinkar to repeat a line in order to answer the old woman. Dinkar quickly repeats it, which satisfies his new old mother. The old woman complains that Aaftaab hasn't changed one bit. Earlier also he used to speak as less as required, and it continues until this day.

She tells the nurse that she is hungry and asks for today's menu. The faces of the nurse and Arisha light up with joy as she had expressed a desire to eat on her own in a long time, whereas before they had to beg her to eat and other times just feed her glucose through her veins.

Arisha calls for Saqina to serve biryani quickly to her grandmother lest her mind changes her. The nurse and Arisha help her to get upright and stuff pillows behind her to support her fragile backbone. A bed table is placed in front of her, and Saqina serves her a plateful of biryani along with raita. She savours spoon after spoon as everyone watches in delight as if she were a baby who just learned to eat by herself. She asks Dinkar to come and have a bite from her hand. Dinkar has always been disgusted to eat food that has touched someone else's lips, and it makes him fidgety. He pretends he did not understand and excuses himself to go to the loo. I wonder if he had done the same in case Arisha had offered him a bite from her plate.

After finishing with her food, Arisha's grandmother makes another wish. She asks to be taken out in the garden, and it's received with open arms. She hasn't been off her bed for months and Dinkar's presence has proved to be miraculous for her. The nurse takes her out in the open, aided by Arisha, in the wheelchair while Dinkar waits in the loo for the old woman to finish food as he is afraid he may contract one of the many diseases she is suffering from if he eats her pickings.

Soon Dinkar joins them too, wearing a jacket as the sun has turned down the heat. They watch the reddened sun go down behind the mountains and darkness crawl up from the opposite side followed by a proliferating procession of stars. As they prepare to take the old woman inside, Altaaf returns home and is pleasantly surprised to see his mother upright, out in the garden.

'Ya Allah, thanks a million times,' he praises.

'Abbu, she had biryani too, which she asked for herself,' tells Arisha with excitement.

'Really?' he utters in disbelief. 'This is Allah's miracle!'

Altaaf goes to Dinkar and gives a pat on his back with a heavy hand in exuberance. Dinkar's tender body feels it like an assault, and his back will carry the imprint of that hand for a long time, but he could not do anything other than smile.

After the dinner, everyone head to their respective rooms. Dinkar asks Saqina for a pen and a notebook, which she provides. Saqina had prepared Dinkar's room like that of a hotel. The king-sized bed is neatly made up with a blanket tucked inside. Thankfully, he has an attached bath/toilet here, and he won't have to wander outside in the morning. Two towels and toiletries are arranged near the wash basin. There is no minibar and television in his room, but he does not need them any which way. Dinkar writes a few couplets and later fantasizes about Arisha. Nothing carnal, just romance. Sleeping on a double bed alone does make one feel lonely, as Dinkar wanders from side to side during the night.

Chapter 16

What a Coincidence

Dinkar wakes up late the next day. It's even more difficult to get out of the blanket in cold weather. Once he finishes with breakfast, it's time for him to entertain his so-called mother with his performance. She has been asking about him since she woke up. Altaaf has already left for work. He and Arisha gather in her room as his mother sits there on her bed. As always, her jaw widens and eyes shrink in elation upon catching a glimpse of her beloved son. But her heart aches at the cold response she has been receiving from him.

'Unna ne kutteya te ni tainu? [Did they beat you up?]' she asks Dinkar.

'Apko maara to nahin unhone?' Arisha translates as she titters. There are some people whose funny bones are too sensitive. Arisha is one of them.

'Nai ji Nai [No, no],' Dinkar refutes it right away.

'Pher 'But' kyun baneya firda e! [Then why do you roam like a dummy!]' scolds the old lady.

Arisha just struggles to translate as she tries to control the tickling inside her and holds her hand tightly over her mouth.

Nevertheless, Dinkar gets it but doesn't react. After hearing a lecture from the mother on the importance of food and good health, Dinkar and Arisha come out and hang in the living room.

'No college today?' asks Dinkar.

'No. DLP,' she replies.

'Data loss prevention?' confirms Dinkar.

'Distance learning programme. I study from home,' scoffs Arisha as she rolls her eyes.

'So what interests you other than studies?' Dinkar tries to divert.

'I love reading shayari!' says Arisha.

'Amen,' says Dinkar to himself as he was anticipating the same reply. It is as if he put words in her mouth. Shayari is his only forte, and he can make any girl go weak in her knees and fall in his arms; at least that is what he muses.

'What a coincidence! I write shayari,' Dinkar proclaims, indulging in euphoria.

'What a coincidence! Aaftaab chachu wrote shayari too! Wait! I will bring his diary.' Arisha is enthralled to learn about their common interests and runs inside to fetch the diary, while Dinkar wonders if his life is anything more than a series of coincidences!

She brings an old diary with a dusty black leather cover and hands it over to Dinkar. He tries to match the impressions of Arisha's fingers imprinted in the dust as he holds the diary. He is daunted to open it. What if a ghazal, which he has written, appears inside the diary? That would confirm his reincarnation as it would be difficult to dismiss it as another coincidence. He opens the diary slowly with raised heartbeat. After peeking inside, he closes it and hands it back to Arisha with a deep sigh.

'It's in Urdu,' he mutters.

'So? You can write shayari in Urdu but you cannot read it?' asks Arisha.

'No. I understand Urdu, but I cannot read and write in Urdu. I write Urdu, but in roman script,' explains Dinkar.

'Oh okay!' says Arisha, cracking the conundrum.

'Never mind. I'll recite it for you,' says Arisha, opening the diary to her favourite page marked by an old peacock feather.

In a matter of a few minutes, Dinkar is reduced from a performing artist to a mere audience. He wants it so hard to recite his ghazal and impress Arisha and finds it difficult to wait any longer. The feeling is the same as if someone wants to pee urgently but is not allowed to. What if his ghazal appears to be a dud in front of Aaftaab's ghazal? What if they are the same? He unwillingly gives a go ahead to Arisha.

'Irshaad,' he says.

Arisha recites as she reads from the diary, and as is the tradition, Dinkar showers praises after each and every couplet.

Parwaanon ki saakh par uthne lage sawaal,

Ik pal ke liye shamaa tanhaa kya hui.

The reputation of the moths is at stake,

As the flame stood lonely for a little while.

Sazaa dene ki usne zehmat bhi na ki,

Hum ye jaan na paaye, khata kya hui.

She did not go through the trouble of punishing me,

And I'll never know where I did err.

Vo mulaqaat kya bas ik ranj thi,

Ibtidaa-e-ishq ki jaane wajah kya hui?

That one meeting was full of animosity,

Wonder what sparked the fire of love.

Peene lagi hai ab vo saath baith kar,

Ik roz maikhaane me saaqi rusvaa kya hui.

She has started drinking alongside me,

Once a bargirl was dishonoured one day.

Raat ki shokhi mein kar baithe vaade hazaar,

Vo sochte hain anjaam, bas subah kya hui.

She made a thousand promises in the tipsiness of the night,

She contemplates the consequences as soon as the dawn breaks.

Deedaar to kiya hota zaraa kafan uthaa kar,

Is kadar bhi mujhse tu khafaa kya hui.

You could have at least taken one last look moving the shroud,

What made you estranged from me to this extent?

Tadapne ko bhi baaki rahe na 'Aaftaab'

Jo jaan hi na lele, phir adaa kya hui.

Aaftaab should not be left over to even squirm,

What good is your swagger, if it doesn't take my life?

'Waah, waah! Beautiful! Too good!' praises Dinkar.

'Shukriya!' says Arisha jokingly, as if it were her creation.

The competition is tough, so Dinkar picks his best creation from the shelf of his memory in the store of his mind.

'Okay, now my turn!' says Dinkar, like a child eager to tell a newly learnt rhyme.

'Irshaad,' says Arisha.

'Arz kiya hai,' recites Dinkar.

Kya bataaun ye kya tishnagi si hai,

Tu saath hai par teri kami si hai.

How do I explain this thirst,

I miss you while you are still with me.

Dinkar takes a little pause, waiting for response from Arisha, but she doesn't react. He proceeds further anyways.

Yun to basti ho tum meri saanson mein,

Dil phir bhi kahe ajnabi si hai.

You float in the air I breathe,

Still you are a stranger to the heart.

He looks at her face, and it's still blank. No 'waah waah' or any sort of comment. That is considered actually rude as one should admire every couplet even if he or she doesn't understand. That's the unwritten constitution of *mushaira*, or social gathering of poets. Dinkar thinks that possibly the people in this country save it for the last and do not interrupt the poet. He recites further, a bit disappointed.

Kuchh hayaa hai teri, kuchh gairat meri,

Andaaz-e-mohabbat mein ik bebasi si hai.

It's your bashfulness and my modesty,

That we are not able to express love freely.

Still no response from her. Dinkar is not able to hold himself any further and asks, 'Are you not getting them or what?'

'Sehar pe ikhtiyaar hai shab-e-suroor ka, Aatish-e-"Aaftaab" mein ghuli "Chandni" si hai,' quotes Arisha as Dinkar gets the shock of his life.

He looks at her in disbelief, holding his breath and trying to wake up from the dream. 'Is it . . . is it in the diary?' asks Dinkar, stumbling upon words in a febrile voice, as drums played in his heart.

Arisha gives him a probing look, swaying her head side to side like a kid trying to find a hidden image in a 3D sticker.

'Ye umr aur ye soch! [Such deep thoughts in this tender age!]' she says.

'Chandniiii!' cries Dinkar in utter dubiety, with widened eyes. That's the phrase Dinkar and Chandni often quoted while chatting to admire each other.

'Dinkar Chauhan!' Arisha giggles nervously.

Chapter 17

Happiness Is Just a Myth

Dinkar is thrilled and simultaneously confused to discover that Arisha is Chandni, the only girl he ever knew and ever loved without even having met. But reality is more captivating than the imagination. He so wanted to meet her, and destiny landed him straight in her home across the border. He is so happy that she is prettier than he could ever imagine.

'But you said you were from Mumbai?' asks Dinkar with a wrinkled forehead.

'Who gives away her real name and location on chatting? Moreover, you wouldn't have chatted with me if I had said 17 f PoK!' tells Arisha.

'I would have chatted with you even if you had told 17 f Somalia!' defends Dinkar. 'So that means everything was false and fake about that chatting!' says Dinkar, questioning her credibility.

'Not at all. Everything was real except my name and location. I am not Chandni Khan but Arisha Sheikh, that's all.' Arisha puts to rest all his allegations.

'Where did you disappear for so long in between?' asks Dinkar.

'There were no signals due to an earthquake. All lines were dead!' tells Arisha as Dinkar remembers that there indeed was an earthquake while he was on the terrace that day with Jahanvi and Mayank.

'And what was that going to a prostitute all about?'

It's now Dinkar's turn to face the trial. 'No, no. That was my crazy cousin Mayank who tried to sabotage me and made it up. When I tried to explain to you, the computer got hanged,' lies Dinkar.

'I see,' says Arisha, accepting his contortion of the facts.

'So are we good?' asks Dinkar.

'I don't know about you, but I am the best!' Arisha laughs as Dinkar provides the chorus.

'Hey, you told me you love to dance! So when can I see your performance?' asks Dinkar.

'On my wedding!' chortles Arisha again.

'I am serious!' Dinkar begins to get irritated by her imbecile behaviour.

'I am serious too. My wedding is in December,' informs Arisha, concealing her discontentment beneath her smile.

'Oh . . . kay.' Dinkar goes numb, not knowing what to say or what to feel, as if every organ inside his body observed a one-minute silence for him. It is like finding a bottle of rare, expensive vintage wine but not having the tool to uncork it while the wine inside the bottle begs you to taste it. His Love Airlines is grounded before even taking off! He undertakes a perilous journey in an unconscious pursuit of her just to dance on her wedding? What is God up to? He falls in an emotional abyss.

'You could at least say congrats!' says Arisha, rescuing him.

'Well, congrats! So who's the lucky guy?' asks choked up Dinkar.

'His name is Sadiq. He is an army officer,' tells Arisha, devoid of any exhilaration.

'Looks like you are not happy,' says Dinkar.

'I don't know! I mean life will be good and all, but he is twelve years older. Feels like I am marrying an uncle,' Arisha opens up to Dinkar and conveys her innermost feelings, which she kept to herself until now, like they used to do while chatting. She shows him Sadiq's picture in her phone.

'He looks all right to me. Just a little bearded!' tells Dinkar.

'Yes! Exactly! But I like clean-shaven guys!' cries Arisha, stamping her feet.

'So why did you agree then?' asks Dinkar.

'Who asked me? I was the last one to be informed about my own engagement!' Arisha grumbles.

'Oh, I see! But you are the positive one, remember? I am sure your married life will be full of bliss!' Dinkar tries to cheer her up.

'There are some situations in life, Dinkar, when no matter how hard you try, you are not able to cast a positive spell on them. You just have to wither through them. In my case, it's my whole remaining life.' Arisha sighs.

Dinkar could not believe she is the same Chandni who appeared so vivacious and positive a few months back. He can do nothing except feel sorry for her as well as himself. Maybe eternal happiness is just a myth that is exalted in fairy tales and movies, he ponders.

'You must have written something new since we chatted last,' says Arisha.

'Yes, I have,' tells Dinkar.

'Phir Irshaad mere huzoor! [Then recite, my sir!]' says Arisha, reminding him of olden times.

'Sure. Arz kiya hai.' Dinkar recites his latest creation, which he conceived last night, and Arisha goes gaga over every couplet unlike the previous one.

Kuchh khilegaa nahin yahan kaanton ke siwa,

Ae baadal tu sehraa mein barastaa hai kyun?

Nothing will flourish here except the thorns,

O mighty cloud, why do you pour in the desert?

Dafn kar chuke jo raaz hum sadiyon pehle,

Aaj zubaan pe aane ko machalta hai kyun?

The secret that I had long buried,

Why does it flutter on my tongue today?

Barson se nahi khilaa ek bhi phool jahan,

Woh gulshan tere aane pe mehaktaa hai kyun?

No flower has blossomed in this garden since ages,

How does it exude fragrance upon your arrival?

Kuchh kami chhod di qatl karne me tune,

Ye dil kabr me bhi dhadaktaa hai kyun?

You erred somewhere while you murdered me,

Why does this heart still beat inside the grave?

Ye adaa hai tumhari ya khuda ka karishmaa,

Mujhe dekh kar tera naqaab saraktaa hai kyun?

Is this your style or God's miracle?

Why does your veil slip upon my one glimpse?

Chhod kar ye haseen vaadiyan ae 'Dinkar',

Tu udaasiyon ke samandar me bhatakta hai kyun?

Instead of these beautiful hills o 'Dinkar',

Why do you wander in a sea of melancholia?

'Too good! Subhaan Allah!' praises Arisha. 'So now you use your original name?'

'Yes. I am not comfortable with Aaftaab any more,' says Dinkar. 'But please don't tell your dad as I am not allowed to reveal my real name!'

'Don't worry! But how did you end up here? You found me at last!' jokes Arisha.

'Itni shiddat se maine tumhe paane ki koshish ki hai, Ke har zarre ne mujhe tumse milaane ki saazish ki hai.' (I have tried to seek you so ardently, that every particle has conspired to unite us.) Dinkar repeats a dialogue from a popular Bollywood movie.

'Oye hoye Shahrukh Khan,' pokes Arisha teasingly as Dinkar's cheek redden.

Dinkar narrates to Arisha his entire harrowing yet exciting tale right from where they left chatting until his landing in PoK.

'Wow! I am sorry you had to go through all this because of my father,' pleads Arisha after listening to his series of misfortunes.

'Well, don't! Because I am happy, he took me out of that mess,' says Dinkar.

'So you don't miss your uncle and aunt?' asks Arisha.

'Nope,' says Dinkar without thinking twice.

'You are made of stone!' she deplores.

'Hmmmm,' agrees Dinkar.

Their fondness for each other grows with every passing day, and they spend hours chattering, laughing, and teasing each other. Sometimes they are so lost in each other that they ignore the calls of the old lady. He tells her about the life in Delhi, their culture, and the festivals, while she informs him of her side. They discuss everything from politics to Bollywood, from religion to reforms, from music to cricket. How the two countries are so similar yet so animus. They also analyse the merits in case the partition had not taken place. How invincible the cricket team would have been? Sometimes in the process, they would step on each other's ego and end up quarrelling as on the issue of Kashmir. Then soon they would reconcile too.

As one poet has rightly said,

"Dil-o-Dimaag muttafiq na hue hind-o-pak ki tarah,

Ye mohabbat mujhe maslaa-e-kashmir lagti hai."

The heart and mind could not agree like India and Pakistan,

This love affair appears to be a Kashmir issue.

Arisha has been the only source of happiness in Dinkar's life, and he is her last shot at happiness before she gets passively married.

Sometimes they unwittingly bump into each other while the other times they make it appear inadvertent. They begin to enjoy the occasional caress and closeness. He usually asks her a glass of water and feels her soft hands while grabbing the glass. As a result, his water intake has increased, but his kidneys are happy to bear the pressure. She often blows in his ear softly from behind to startle him when no one is looking, sending tickles down his spine. Soon they begin to jar in the eyes of Saqina, whom Altaaf had entrusted with the job of keeping an eye on Dinkar.

November arrives, and the region witnesses its first snowfall of the season, but for Dinkar, the first of his life. The people carry a kangri, a portable fire pot filled with red hot ambers under the pheran which provides them respite from the harsh weather. The entire landscape is covered in snow. It's beautiful and serene, yet it resembles someone draped in a white shroud beneath which everything lies cold and lifeless. Diwali comes and goes without Dinkar's notice. He celebrates with them Milad-un-Nabi instead as they light up the house in the same way as his house is lit up on Diwali back in India. As for Dinkar, he vowed not to celebrate Diwali as he lost his parents on Diwali eve.

Arisha grows irascible as her wedding date nears. It is to coincide with her birthday, which incidentally is Dinkar's birthday too. Dinkar has contemplated eloping with Arisha many times, but he could not suggest the idea to her as he knows that even if she agrees, he does not have the required guts to execute the plan. It would have been another suicide mission, more or less. The other reason is that Dinkar does not want to betray Altaaf. The affectionate love and care of the old woman and companionship of Arisha he received in his house fills him with gratitude towards Altaaf. Not once did he feel the need of his antidepressants. But as December approaches, he feels the need. Recently, Arisha has started to distance herself from him. The bouts of depression have been hitting him since. He thinks of committing suicide sometimes, but a glimpse of Arisha changes his mind. What would he do once she gets married? Who will stop him then?

Chapter 18

The Seventy-Two Virgins

One not so fine morning in early December, Altaaf knocks on Dinkar's door repeatedly. As Dinkar opens the door, Altaaf appears edgy and asks Dinkar to dress up and pack his stuff, which he accumulated here. He hands him over a bag and waits outside. Dinkar looks at the wall clock, and the minute hand still has a quarter of a circle to cover in order to strike six. He fears Saqina has spilled the beans and Altaaf is kicking him out. He goes to the bathroom and splashes some icy cold water in his eyes in order to wake up fully. After twenty minutes, he comes out of his room, fully dressed according to the snowy conditions with his bag stuffed. He can hear Arisha crying inconsolably in an adjacent room. Each of her shrieks pierces his heart like a dagger. He wants to go and hug her, but Altaaf doesn't even allow him to bid adieu to her and his mother. He doesn't know whether he will be able to see Arisha again or not but finds himself helpless. Altaaf tells him that it's time to leave and steps out of the house. He quietly follows Altaaf with his feet sinking in the snow, feeling the weight of his guilt as he thinks he has betrayed the trust of Altaaf. A van waits in front of their gate on the road. Dinkar boards the van, and

Altaaf orders his driver to proceed. Dinkar watches Altaaf regretfully, receding away through the foggy windows as the van proceeds slowly on the icy winding road downhill.

'Where are you taking me?' Dinkar asks Bashir. He is the same person who met him at the guest house.

'Your job is over in Altaaf bhai's house,' replies Bashir.

'What job? I don't understand!' asks Dinkar.

'Altaaf bhai's mother passed away in her sleep this morning,' says Bashir.

Dinkar is stunned by the news. His vision goes blurry as his eyes are flooded with an unexpected tsunami of tears. A part of him is confused too as if asking why this sudden well up? He hardly cared for her. As the van proceeds further and further away from the house, he is blitzed with her memories. How she held his hand, kissed his forehead, tried to feed him, smiled upon his one glimpse, and constantly begged him to eat. And as we all feel guilt-ridden from time to time upon a demise of a close old relative, Dinkar too is contrite for not spending time with her when he could. Suddenly he misses his aunt and uncle too and wants to tell the driver to drop him at Lajpat Nagar, but this wasn't a Delhi cab. Although this is all ephemeral, what's everlasting is the hollow in his chest as his heart is still there with Arisha. Now he feels that Altaaf threw him out like an unwanted child born out of wedlock. All his gratefulness for Altaaf goes out the window. His curiosity about the destination dies down. After grieving for an hour and a half, he notices that the view outside has changed from hilly to flat just like his lifeline. The snow has disappeared, and there's greenery all around. The weather is comparatively warm, but his hands and feet are still cold. The sun occasionally peeps through the small windows in the clouds.

The van leaves the highway and takes a narrow dusty road through the bushes. It comes to a halt as the road is blocked by a huge horizontal iron bar, as if it were an army check post. It's guarded by armed men in military uniform. Bashir alights and greets them. He appears to frequent here often. He shows them some papers that are probably some sort of identification. A guard carrying a rifle comes near the van and closely inspects its trunk. Then he takes a good look at Dinkar. After a minute, he signals the other guard, and the bar is lifted. The van proceeds inside for about one kilometre and comes to stop in front of a huge gate beyond which the private vehicles are not allowed. It looks like an army training area and is heavily guarded and fenced all around. Two guards on either side of the gate stand behind a pile of sandbags with RPGs mounted on top. Another two guard the gate on foot with rifles. Bashir and Dinkar get out of the van with his stuff and proceed towards a small window alongside the gate, resembling a ticket window of a movie theatre. An intermittent round of bullets being fired can be heard nearby. Dinkar is devoid of any excitement or fear. He left his emotions behind in that house.

Bashir hands over the papers inside from a small opening like that of Jerry's home in *Tom and Jerry*. A guard carries a thorough search of Dinkar's bag. Afterwards a small opening inside the big gate opens up, and they enter. As he walks inside along with Bashir, it becomes clear that it is indeed a training area with many men being trained at a distance. Some running around, some climbing on ropes, some crawling under the wires, and others engaged in target practice. On proceeding closer, Dinkar discovers that they are young lads not less than twelve and not more than sixteen years old. There is a small mosque with a loudspeaker on its minaret and a covered praying area along with two barracks. Bashir takes him to a small building, which looks like an office. He hands him over to a guy named Bakhtaawar Khan along with the paperwork. Bakhtaawar welcomes Dinkar zealously, as if he were an old acquaintance. Bashir takes their leave.

'Welcome, Aaftaab, welcome!' greets Bakhtaawar.

Bakhtaawar's face glows under a neatly tucked layered round turban partially covering his burgundy hairs, and his beard too is of the same colour as if dyed with henna. He is a tall fellow who looks debonair in his brown pathani suit with a black jacket on top, giving an impression of a high-ranked executive with his style. He is not as young as he appears as he should be at least fifty to be in this position. He has retired from fieldwork as is evident by his limping. Bakhtaawar is one of the managers here and a close associate of Altaaf, who is chief recruiter of this camp. He is aware of the real identity of Dinkar. They both believe that if Dinkar thinks he is Aaftaab, then he could be used on a mission. If not, he could be easily expended any time. Bakhtaawar's job is to find out if he is fit for a mission, mentally as well as physically.

Bakhtaawar shows him his room, which is basically a storeroom inside the office. Dinkar is receiving special treatment due to his complicated background. All the other boys stay in a barrack in bunks. He will not be allowed to mix with them until he is ready or, in other words, brainwashed fully.

'So, Aaftaab, do you know why you are here?' asks Bakhtaawar.

'No,' says Dinkar, as he puts his bag under a small bed.

'Altaaf is now beginning to believe that you are his lost brother,' Bakhtaawar tries to manipulate him.

'Oh! So that's why he did not even allow me to pay last respect to my own mother?' Dinkar questions his intention.

'No, my friend, you don't understand!' explains Bakhtaawar. 'Altaaf sent you away because soon his house will be flocked with relatives and friends for mourning, and he doesn't want to answer their questions regarding you as you know it's complicated.'

Dinkar is not ready to buy that story. 'So what do you want me to do?' asks Dinkar.

'If you say you are Aaftaab, then you have to prove your allegiance to his faith, his country, and his people,' tells Bakhtaawar.

Dinkar is dead inside after parting from Arisha for the second time. First was when he lost her online. Now he just wants to end his life as he sees no hope of returning to Arisha. Another ten days and she will be a married woman. His life has lost its purpose. He thinks he has seen enough and nothing in this world will ever bless him with joy again, the way Arisha did. Her fond memories won't be able to drag the load of his disappointments for long. He is too tired of the unending misery, of the omnipotent pain, and the omnipresent dejection. He has chosen his fate.

'How about a suicide mission? Would it prove my allegiance?' asks Dinkar.

'Allah be praised! It will. It will!' says Bakhtaawar, smiling in exuberance as if he witnessed a miracle. He is more than happy as Dinkar cut his job by half. What better way to get rid of him than to use him for their shoddy motives. Now all he has to do is to convert him to Islam.

'But you have to first embrace Islam,' says Bakhtaawar.

'No problem! But I won't get circumcised!' Dinkar sets a condition.

'There is no such obligation, my friend,' says Bakhtaawar, laughing heartily.

He calls for the imam of the mosque. The imam has different meanings in Sunni and Shia sects. In Sunni Islam, imam is the one who leads prayer in a mosque, but in Shiite Islam, imam is the religious head. The imam arrives shortly, and Bakhtaawar informs him about Dinkar's desire to convert to Islam. The imam welcomes his decision and gives him a brief overview of the religion and its beliefs before the conversion. Then he asks him if he is ready to fully submit himself to the will of God. Dinkar gives his readiness at once. The imam then asks him to recite after him the shahada, an oral declaration of faith, after which one becomes Muslim.

'La ilaha illallah, Muhammadun rasulullah.'

'There is no god other than Allah and Muhammad [prophet] is his messenger.'

As soon as Dinkar repeats after him, Bakhtaawar and the imam congratulate him. The imam tells him that from now on, he will be called Muhammad Aaftaab. He also informs him that it's equivalent to his rebirth and that he will be free of all his former sins and advises him to take a bath of purification. He advises him to visit the mosque later where he will further sermonize on the principles of Islam and its way of life. Dinkar follows his advice and takes a shower in the bathroom attached to the office. He visits the mosque afterwards, where the imam further teaches him about the fard, or Islamic obligations; adab, or Muslim etiquettes; and about the Koran, which will continue every day. He also tells him about the importance of five daily prayers, or namaz, and how and when to perform them. He already knows most of it from Arisha.

After going through the session at the mosque, Dinkar feels a providential tranquillity inside him similar to the one you receive in any spiritual place, be it a temple, a gurdwara, or a church.

Bakhtaawar asks Dinkar to take the rest of the day off as he must be reeling under the loss of his loved one. For a moment, Dinkar is staggered as to how Bakhtaawar knew about him and Arisha. Then he realizes that he must be referring to the mother as the loved one. Dinkar spends the rest of the day in his petite room surrounded by recollections of Arisha. Lunch is served to him in his room by a young boy who is hardly twelve years old. He greets Aaftaab and introduces himself as Ahmad and hands him a plate full of rice and chicken curry poured on top.

'I hear you are from India,' the boy asks.

'Yes,' says Dinkar as he begins to eat.

'Have you seen Salman Khan?' he asks with zest.

'No,' says Dinkar. The boy's excitement fizzes away like the carbon dioxide from the soft drink bottle.

'Are you here for a mission?' asks the boy.

'Yes, a suicide mission. Boom!' Dinkar says animatedly to scare him away.

'Wow! You are so lucky,' says the lad in an envious tone.

It was Dinkar's turn to be scared now. He looks at the boy in a daze. He could not believe his ears. *Who fed him that?* he thinks.

'See you in paradise!' says Ahmad and runs away as if he had an important errand to run.

The next day begins early with the morning prayer before sunrise followed by a two-hour-long sermon emphasizing on the rewards of submitting to the will of God. After breakfast, boys undergo rigorous training, breaking intermittently for prayers and meals. They dress in green pathani suits with round woollen caps and jackets. The boys play with the real guns in the age when they should be playing with toy guns.

Dinkar doesn't need much training as he has to learn only to press a button. He maintains distance from rest of them except during prayers. He spends rest of the time meditating in the mosque as he finds temporary relief there from his inner turmoil.

Evening is reserved for the movies, not the Hollywood or Bollywood ones but gorywood movies that show brutalities and causalities suffered on the part of the Muslim world, blaming the West and even India in order to stir the young minds for jihad, or holy war, against them. After the video session, the commander asks the boys, 'Who is ready to go on a suicide mission to avenge these brutalities?' Each of them raises their hand as if he asked for an excursion to Disneyland.

Aaftaab soon becomes a hero in the eyes of the boys of the camp as they learn about his mission through Ahmad. They congratulate him and wish him success in his mission as and when they bump into him. Dinkar too enjoys the attention. Soon he makes a few friends too. He asks them why they chose to be here and all of them had the same reply: for a better life as well as afterlife. Most of the boys are from very poor background, and they are happy that at least they get a plateful to eat and also some money for the family back home. Hunger and poverty takes precedence over faith.

It's five days to go for Arisha's wedding, and Dinkar does not want to live to see the day. Bakhtaawar gives him his good news. His mission is finalised. It's on the Indian side. He has to blow himself up during a rally of Indian prime minister in Srinagar. Though the prime minister is not the target as they are aware that they won't be able to reach anywhere near him. The aim is to create tensions between the two nations in order to thwart the dialogue between their leaders as it does not find favour with fundamentalist organizations here. But it's next month. Bakhtaawar introduces him to one of his commanders, Hamid, who will prepare Dinkar for his mission.

Hamid takes him to the armoury. It looks like a warehouse filled with a pile of boxes. He opens a cabinet and shows him. It is a blue jacket fitted with explosives and a detonator connected with an intricate network of wires and a red trigger.

'Here is your ticket to paradise,' says Hamid.

He picks it up carefully and holds it up against Dinkar's back to check the size like a tailor measuring the size of sherwani on the groom-to-be. Dinkar gets goosebumps as the jacket touches his body. His long haunting nightmare is finally becoming a reality.

Hamid tells him that it's loose for him and it needs to be adjusted. In the meanwhile, he asks him to go through a black and yellow coloured book with the title *Suicide Vest for Dummies*. LOL, I am just kidding. He does not give him any such book as there isn't any because only dummies use suicide vests! Though he explains to him its connections and working in detail. It has four cylinders containing C-4 explosives and shrapnel like nails, nuts, ball bearings, and pieces of thick wires to inflict maximum damage and increase casualties. It is electrically detonated by a red button which, as per Hamid, is the doorbell to paradise.

It's 12 December, and Dinkar has become an expert by now in the use of the suicide vest. Hamid tells him that it's been adjusted to his size. He also informs him that there is a small function tomorrow in the camp, and he should give a demonstration to all the boys about its working. Dinkar agrees without a fuss.

The 13 December arrives, and Dinkar turns seventeen today. It's the birthday and wedding day of Arisha too, and Dinkar is mighty depressed. He tries to imagine how gorgeous she would look in the bridal wear, though his imagination is restricted to the Indian brides in red lehnga. He daydreams where he arrives at her wedding and works out a last-minute switch and marries her, like in many Bollywood movies.

In the afternoon, everyone including the faculty gather in the open for a ceremony. The boys wonder what it is about as they drool over the refreshments and snacks arranged on a long table covered in white sheets with a large box kept in the centre that seems to be housing a cake. Dinkar would have suspected that it's his surprise birthday bash, but he knows that no one is aware of the date here and those are not the norms of this camp. Bakhtaawar hosts the function as he stands on a small raised ground while everyone gathers around him like a pep talk before the cricket match. He begins by informing them that this function is in commemoration of completing the seventeen years of attack on the Indian parliament and to remember the martyrs involved who were trained in this very camp. He adds further that boys of this camp have successfully carried out the 2005 Delhi blasts and 2008 Mumbai attacks, which make him feel very proud.

Wait a minute, did he say 2005 Delhi blasts? Dinkar thinks to himself as if he had awakened from a dream and finally had come to his senses. These were the same blasts that changed his life forever. These were the blasts that took his parents away from him and left him an orphan. The visions from the past play in front of his eyes as if he were transported to the location and time of the incident, and he watches the blast rip through the market. The mutilated bodies of his parents lay before him while his little self cries in the hands of the maid. A river of tears starts flowing down his eyes, and he finds himself back among the boys. Bakhtaawar appears inaudible to him as his ears can only hear the cries and shrieks of the people affected by the blast.

Meanwhile, the celebration continues as a large cake in the shape of the Indian map is unboxed. Dinkar is asked to come forward to cut the cake as he is the next in line of martyrs. Bakhtaawar asks him to cut a piece of Jammu and Kashmir from the rest of India as he hands him over the knife. Dinkar holds the knife with shaky hands as it appears to be soaked and dripping with the blood of innocent Indians that died in various terrorist attacks across the country. His school days memory visits him as every morning they sang 'Jan Gan Man' (national anthem) filled with a bout of patriotism and the yearly Independence Day and Republic Day parades he used to take part in. He saluted the tricolour countless times during rehearsals but each time with the renewed vigour and zeal.

He still goes ahead with slicing the head of the cake like carving his own heart out of his chest as the shrieks and cries of people in his own head grow louder. The cake is immediately sent for the boys to feast upon. The faces of the young boys surrounding him transform into live ticking bombs with names of various cities of India labelled over them as they devour the parts of India. He is appalled by the mere thought of destruction and havoc that these bombs will wreak in future and the countless Dinkars they will produce.

Now it's his turn to give a demo to the boys on the use of the suicide vest post which he will be felicitated and saluted for his mission. Dinkar climbs the elevated ground as Hamid opens the box he carries and reveals the vest. The excitement of the boys culminates to a new high as if he has revealed the iPhone 10.

Dinkar overflows with emotions mainly comprising of guilt and anger. He deeply regrets agreeing to such an endeavour for selfish motives and not caring about the innocent lives that will be lost in the process. *"What was I thinking? What had gotten inside me? How could I be so shallow and inconsiderate? That too after being a victim of it whole my life?"*, he contemplates in self-reproach. Simultaneously, he is infuriated at the camp and its comrades as they murdered his parents and turned his life into a damnation.

Nevertheless, he proceeds with his training as Hamid helps him wear the vest hand-stitched to his size. Hamid explains the donning of the suicide vest to the curious boys. He ties its buckles on Dinkar's back tightly and then hands over to him to explain its operation.

'My dear friends, as you can see, I am wearing this suicide vest. Its operation is very simple,' explains Dinkar. 'You just have to switch on the power here at the side and then press this red trigger. Allahu Akbar [God is greatest] and Jay Hind [Salutation towards India]!'

Next day, all the major regional newspapers report on the front page: A commander in a training camp accidentally explodes his suicide vest, killing at least eighty people.

Dinkar finally committed suicide, not for himself but for his country—a martyrdom that his countrymen will never hear or read about anywhere, nor will he be given any medal or any petrol pump. There won't be any road named after him, nor any statue of him erected on an intersection. There won't be any Facebook posts in his name demanding likes or any condolence tweets. Neither will his country rejoice over the fact that so many potential bombs have been diffused before they could have been activated. For them, he is still a traitor, a liar, and an absconder. No one will ever know for sure whether he was Aaftaab or not, but if he really was, then his pursuit of paradise and seventy-two virgins ended in this terror factory in his second innings as seventy-two young lads died, all virgins.